The Ice Arrows

Aylie Fucella

Illustrated by Alisdair Wright

Copyright © 2013 Aylie Fucella

Illustration copyright © 2013 Alisdair Wright

All rights reserved.

ISBN: 1490470719

ISBN-13: 978-1490470719

CONTENTS

Contents iii

Prologue 5

She Arrives 6

Reads Minds 11

The Legend 14

My Destiny 17

The Snake Entrance 23

Harry's Story 26

Flying Fire 33

Understanding Fire Power 37

Pie and an Accident 41

GG! 46

Busy Roads and Busy Rats 53

Split Up 63

Song in the Blissful Light 68

Psychic Dreams and up a Hill 72

Climbing down and Erupting Up 77

Animals and Freaky Dreams 83

Cliff jumping 86

The Vast 91

Evil Seaweed 97

Luca 102

Anusha	106
Minties Want our Bodies	110
Ticker, Sailor, Soldier, Die	115
Fire and Time	121
A Broken Heart and an Escape	126
Faking Death in front of Ghosts	130
Paper Thin	134
Moving On and Awkward Songs	136
Fireworks	139
Sand, Sand and more Sand	142
Captured by the Wind	146
Lost and Hungry	149
Disappointment	153
Our First Meeting	156
I Have Some Talent	160
Showdown, Bolts and Bat-eries	163
GG Found	174
The Carnivorous cave	181
I Am the Flame	183
Shooting	186
Home	190

PROLOGUE

I never believed in legends, myths, or even stories for that matter. To my mind they were just pieces of paper covered in the longings of a lonely writer, a sorry excuse for an imaginative person who has nothing to do but write, write, write. Boring. I thought it just showed they had no self-confidence and no friends. I would rather do something with my life, be somebody. But now, I do believe, I have to believe in stories. And pretty strongly, I'll tell you that. This is my story.

SHE ARRIVES

I sat up straight in my bed, on an early morning in June, as the cockerel crowed. I had already been awake for hours, my mind buzzing with thoughts about the day ahead; ready to take it on. The news had arrived a week ago from the social services. After seven years of searching through files and sorting through millions of potentially related people, I couldn't believe they had actually found her. My heart beat like a marching band drum as I raced around the small room, getting ready. I strapped on my overalls and fell over putting on my only pair of scruffy old boots. Usually I wear shorts, a baggy sweatshirt that can get dirty and sneakers that I can run around in for training. But today, I wanted to look extra special.

The short distance over to the deserted main tent of the long gone circus, was a blur, as I ran like a maniac towards my destination.

The sun was burning like fire. Even though it was humid and I was perspiring like a pig, a chill of excitement rolled down my spine, along with sweat. I entered the tent, an inch of my body at a time, not wanting to make any noise. It didn't take long for me to realize that I was holding my breath, because I started gagging and gulping in the disgusting air. Oops. There goes trying not to make any noise. My last relative was somewhere in this smoky tent, waiting for me to run to her and hug her and tell her how long I'd been hoping for someone to come along. The mysterious disappearance of my parents was too much to handle for a five year old girl with a perfect life. I couldn't help being a little bit angry with her. I mean, where had she been the whole of my childhood? I searched the room, straining my eyes to find her through the thick pipe smoke.

But she wasn't there. I tried calling but there was no answer. I knew it was hopeless, she wasn't in the tent. My heart sank and the emptiness of another disappointment swept over me. My last connection had bailed on me and there was nothing I could do about it. I felt so stupid for trusting someone who may have been a figment of my imagination, or just a lie.

I left the tent, my head bowed, and my expression still devastated. As soon as I walked out of that tent, the answer to the question that had been floating in the back of my mind; where was all the pipe smoke coming from, greeted me. Jamal Neressi, the possibly psychotic fortune teller was smoking his extremely long, ivory pipe, while sitting in a giant lawn chair with a book in his hand. He had been staying with the shoemaker ever since the circus closed. I couldn't help letting out a little snicker. He looked hilarious, sitting there reading 'The Secrets to Fortune Telling and Why they should be kept Secret', with his giant pot belly and his red and gold turban. He looked over and gave me a stern glare as if to say, "Get the blazes out of my sun, you little twerp." I quickly turned away and went back to my sulking.

"Well, that didn't take very long. What happened? Did those idiotic service people get it wrong?" Lola Moar was waiting outside the circus arena, leaning against an empty microphone stand that had shouted out the show times a few weeks before. My protector didn't like ordinary people without the military training she had. In fact, she didn't really like anyone. Or at least she didn't portray 'like' towards anybody. Her scars told her story. She was in the military for a very long time, in the war against Zoal. I didn't know what this war was about, nobody would tell me. Anyway, she was chosen to be my guardian after my parents left. Lola (stupid name for her, who would pick Lola for a big, scary army freak) was supposed to educate and take care of me. She was also supposed to help me figure out the mystery behind the key that had hung around my neck since my parents had put it on me when I was a baby. They had always said that I would unravel the mystery when I turned fifteen, so two more years to go.

I nodded my head slowly. "Yes, ma'am. She's not in there." I whispered, my throat still sore from gagging smoke. I could feel little beads of sweat running down my face. I knew it was sweat because I never cry. Never. Especially not in front of anyone. And especially not in front of Lola. She would make me do fifty pushups or something. I shrugged my shoulders and quickly sidled off, hoping Lola wouldn't call me back to bark at me for being so weak, or make me do the training course, since there was now no reason for having the day off. But she didn't say anything; she just looked at me as I walked away with the weirdest expression on her face. It looked like...no, it couldn't have been... it looked like sympathy. Sympathy! From Lola! Wow, this was definitely going in the record books.

I wondered if she *was* going to give me the full day off. Usually, I wake up at dawn and start a few lessons. Now Lola, being how she is, didn't really care about school smarts, like English or maths or music. She had thrown the home-schooling books the Social Services gave us to the back of the cupboard. The only thing she ever really taught me was what she knew, and learned at boot camp and in the war; strategy, survival, weapons and, my favorite, self-defense. Lola set up a whole assault course in the back yard for me. Every day she would make me do the course, over and over again until I was able to do it in under a minute. And let me tell you, I haven't ever done it on the first go, even with all the practice.

I dragged myself back to the house, thinking about my pathetic little life, that seemed irrelevant compared to everyone else that I knew. I mean, nobody really cared what happened to me after all. My only relative alive didn't care. I trudged up the steps and pushed open the screen door with my head. By the time I realized that Lola had locked the wooden door behind the screen, it was too late. "Ow! Oh, great, just what I need. A giant bump on my head." I mumbled to myself. Isn't talking to yourself one of the first signs of brain damage?

"Oh, are you all right?" A passer-by asked, even though it was obvious that I wasn't.

"It's okay, I'm fine."

"I wonder if you can help me, I'm looking for Miss Lola Moar. I'm supposed to be meeting her at the main tent. The only problem is, well, I can't find it." She chuckled nervously. I looked her up and down. She was old but with a warm and youthful face that was wrinkled from years of smiling. She had a bun of straggly white hair that could have come down to her hips if she released it. Her clothes were a dull grey but upper class in style with satin lacing and a jewel studded pouch. She was hunched over an elegant walking stick waiting for me to respond. She fitted my stereotype of a rich, old granny. Why would anybody want to meet with Lola? She never has visitors. Unless…

My eyes widened and my jaw swung open. "I'm…I'm Alexis B-Blake," I stuttered, trying to hold it together, "Are… are you-"

"Yes, my dear. I am your grandmother. I understand you've been looking for me?"

"Yes, yes! I've been looking for you for a very long time!" I shrieked in delight.

And then I froze. I had found her. Finally, I had not been forgotten.

READS MINDS

Grace and I sat at the kitchen island. You could have cut the silence with a butter knife. We just sat there looking at each other. My face must have been distorted in a really odd way, because I was angry, ecstatic and confused by the fact that this stranger was the same blood as me. I guess it was just so overwhelming, I didn't know how to react. She had come out of nowhere, claiming to be my grandmother and I didn't know how to talk or act in front of her. Finally, she broke the silence.

"So, how's life?" she asked, all smiley. And then I lost it.

"IF YOU HAD BEEN HERE IN THE FIRST PLACE, YOU WOULD KNOW!" I exploded. There was silence again. I didn't even look at her; I reckoned I knew what expression would be on her face.

"I understand."

I was shocked. I looked up to see a sad and caring face staring into my eyes. I think she was *worried* about me. That is another first for the day. Even when I broke my leg coming down the ropes, Lola just bandaged me up and made me do strategy quizzes until I got better.

"W-what do you mean?"

"You think life is miserable. You miss your parents and you don't think anyone cares about you. And most of all, you don't know who to trust. You don't even trust Lola. I bet when you go to sleep at night, you lock your windows and doors. I think I know what your problem is, Alexis. You don't believe in love, you don't even believe in friendship."

Whoa, I was not expecting that. I sat back and pondered on this surprising statement from a stranger. I wondered if she could read my mind.

I leant forward and lowered my voice, "Can you read thoughts?"

She started screaming. I didn't know what was wrong; I thought maybe I should call someone. But when I glanced at her in my panic, I saw that she was laughing, hysterically. In fact, she was almost crying, she was laughing so hard.

"No!" She managed to exclaim between cackles, "No, I studied child psychology at uni, sweet heart!"

I felt like an idiot. I could feel my cheeks burning up and turning bright red. Nobody laughs at me. Ever. Trying to keep my cool, I got down from my seat and went to the fridge and got out two bottles of lemon twist. I slammed one on the counter top in front of her and shimmied back on to my seat. Trying to look as aggressive as I could, I yanked open the pop cap and threw it into the bin. I took a giant gulp of soda and burped loudly. Her face remained in a 'yeah, sure' expression.

"You may proceed." I said in a monotone. "Honey,

you need to believe. If you don't you'll never have anyone. Now, I know you've been looking for me for quite some time, but what were you really looking for? Do you want someone to take care of you? You've got Lola and plus, I won't be around for much longer. Tell me, Miss Blake, what is the true meaning of my being here." She stared into me, waiting for my reply, but already knowing what the answer was. That made one of us.

After another long silence, I braved it. "I don't know, Grace. Maybe it was because I needed reassurance that I am not the last Blake ever, maybe I just needed a family. But the thing is, I don't need a family, I don't need anything, not from you or anyone!" My voice got louder and louder.

"Fine then. I'll leave and the world will end."

"Huh?" I said dumbly.

THE LEGEND

"Sweetheart, may I tell you a story."

"As long as it explains what you just said!" I retorted.

"It starts a long time ago, a very long time ago. Before my great, great grandmother was born, before this city was built. Before the empire was split into two; the Cordons, us, and the Zoalons, the city on the other side of the valley.

There is a legend throughout the land of a terrible, evil, greedy King, who ruled like a tyrant and cut off more heads than a butcher kills pigs. He reigned for twenty years until a humble blacksmith met a beautiful young sorceress and together they hatched a plan to take down the horrible king. She sneaked into the castle under an invisible enchantment while the blacksmith distracted the guards. She quickly crept into the King's chambers and struck him down with a spell to make it look like a heart attack. Even though she was very ashamed of the murder, she knew it was the right thing to do and dreamt of living in love with the blacksmith forever. But, the King's advisor sent out a witch hunter who uncovered her guilt and sought to destroy her. To protect the blacksmith, she cut her heart into three pieces. She then asked her love to craft three Arrows, one of silver, one of bronze and one of gold. In each of the Arrow tips, she placed a piece of her heart. As the heart entered the tips, the Arrows immediately turned to solid ice. She secured them in three faraway places. Only when the master of fire shoots the three heavy Arrows into the target, will the Ice Empress, as she became known, come back to help humanity with her magic.

When Vola, the king's advisor could not find her, he tried to hunt down anyone else in the empire that believed in her and wanted her to rule. This was when the country split in two; the Zoalons were the people who were either too cowardly to stand up for the Ice Empress or they really did hate her. That is the civilization on the other side of the valley. People could no longer trust one another in case a friend turned out to be a Volan spy. Vola does not rule anymore, but his great, great, great grandson, the horrible Zacheri Smoke is the city leader.

The people who were persecuted because they loved the Empress were moved here, to this side of the valley so as to not rub off on the 'good' people there. It was like a prison, working day and night. The abuse they handed out was horrible. They whipped each person every morning and evening and whenever they made even a small mistake. Finally, a man called Memphis Blake decided this was too much and devised a plan to take over the city and rule this land. He managed to restore peace and arranged an agreement that there were to be two cities, and they would never converse again unless completely necessary. The cities have lived happily and well for many years.

But people still remember the prophecy. 'Only when the master of fire shoots the three Arrows into the target will the Ice Empress come back to help humanity with her magic.' Memphis knew this. In fact he knew it very well. He pondered this every night, because he had a secret. Now, don't panic when I tell you this, but he was a fire demon. He had power over fire. And so do you now."

MY DESTINY

"AHHHHHHHHHHHHHH" I woke up screaming. Nightmare demons had been filling my head with freaky pictures of the story. Had yesterday actually happened? Or did I just have an overactive imagination?

"Sweetheart, can I come in? It's your grandmother." That answered that question.

I tried to think of a snappy response to get her to go away, "Um, I'm busy; you'll have to come back later…"

She didn't answer so I thought she had gone. I got out of bed and went to turn on the T.V. but the power was out. "Oh, just perfect," I said out loud, "bloody electricity." I huffed and sat on the edge of my bed, trying to think of something to do. I was most certainly not going to go outside to welcome my grandmother into my life. She had lost her chance already after yesterday's charade. I ran it through in my head from the point where I lost it. There wasn't any reason to go through the whole legend again. I had seen it enough in my dreams.

What a crazy idiot. She expected me to believe this lunacy? What was she trying to get out of me by telling me lies? Maybe she was trying to recruit me for some special society. I had said nothing because I didn't think it would be a good idea to engage in conversation with a maniac. Nodding my head, I had motioned for her to go on, even though I had one of my best, raised-eyebrow looks on.

"Memphis is your great, great, grandfather and the gift has been passed on to you. I do not have the gift; I am only a Blake by marriage. But you do. Memphis never went after the ice Arrows because he believed the Ice Empress's return was unnecessary; he had already made peace. Your great grandfather made the same decision. But twenty-three years ago, your grandfather, Mortimer, realized that with the evil Zacheri Smoke ruling Zoal there could no longer be peace. He travelled all the way to the Carnivorous Cave, only to be struck down by the evil that lies there before he got a chance to shoot the Arrows into the target. You see, if the Arrows are not fired by the one that collected them before he or she dies, they return to their original hiding places. But there is still hope. I loved Mo very much and I followed him throughout his journey. He wrote a journal, you see, of all the dangers and treacheries that he faced. It's like a guide book for anyone else if he didn't…"

"It's okay, you don't have to-"

"No, I do have to tell! The survival of the world is on your shoulders. I'm sorry. May I go on?"

"Um, okay."

"Yes, well, Alexis. I have to tell you something very important now. It's about your parents. I know what happened to them."

My mouth dropped open and hung there. Anyone mentioning my parents would soon know that if they didn't shut up, a right hook would be coming their way. But I couldn't hit her. I'm not that horrible. I couldn't do anything but slump with my mouth open and my eyes wide. 'Miss Alexis Blake has just won the world's Most Surprised Look On Her Face- award' was going through my mind. It was quickly interrupted by the chatter of two loud teenagers walking past the window.

"Let's go somewhere a little more private," Grace suggested.

Before she could get down from her chair I got up, put the blinds down, locked the screen door and checked to make sure no one was in the house.

"Okay, its private now," I said matter-of-factly, "What were you going to say about my parents?"

"Your parents were going to go on the journey. They were going to try and free the Empress. They planned for months and months. You would come live with me while they were gone for a year. But there was a traitor among us. Zacheri Smoke learnt about the plans and he sent one of his goons to… finish the job."

A gob smacked face is never very attractive, not that I care about being pretty. I just couldn't believe it. They didn't leave me, they were killed. Mum and Dad did care about me. But this relief was crushed when I remembered that the person telling me this had probably lost her marbles a long time ago, if you know what I mean. I eventually got control over my face and marbled a neutral expression. Nobody can see through *my* poker face.

"Alexis. You must do what they couldn't. You must find the Arrows and set free the Ice Empress or terrible things will happen." She grabbed my shoulders and looked me right in the eye. I had been staring at a patch on the counter that had a little spilt lemon twist on it.

"Like what?"

"The world will end, chaos will spread throughout the globe, and no one will be safe. Zacheri is planning things, terrible things, in his madness he wants everyone to suffer. The Ice Empress is the only one who can help us save ourselves from the dangers to come."

I was so confused. *Make up your mind, Lexi, do you believe her or not*, I yelled to myself in my head, *is this really true?* Then I had a brainwave.

"Prove it, I mean like real proof. If you just pull out a diary, you could have written it yourself." If this lady was trying to con me, I'd find out.

She didn't say anything in response, but instead, pointed to the door. A boy was standing outside, his hair a dirty brown, like he just swung it in a puddle of mud. Deep brown eyes that had a hint of gold when he looked up. Man, this guy was hot. Not that I'm into stuff like that, just saying. I estimated he was about 14 or so. His tall build was packed with muscles everywhere. *No doubt he has a six pack,* I thought to myself. His honey dipped eyes turned to me as I swerved my head back to Grace.

"Who's the dude?" I asked, jabbing my thumb

towards him.

"My name's Harry," he said awkwardly, "Pleasure to meet you, Miss Alexis."

I swiveled back. His voice so didn't match his looks. It sounded like a seven year old's. What the??? "Uh, nice to meet you, Harry. Would you like some tea and finger sandwiches?" I said in my poshest voice. I cracked up laughing, then realized I was being given the evil eye from GG (Grandma Grace, I think I'll call her that from now on) so I straightened up and walked to the screen door to unlock it for Posh Socks. He strode to GG's side and leaned against the fridge with his hands in his pockets.

"Go on Harry, show her your gift" GG insisted.

He stared at his feet shyly and then lifted his head to stare at me, "What's your favorite animal?"

I raised an eyebrow and just looked at him. "*Seriously?*" My eyebrows said. I decided to play along with his game. "Pterodactyl."

"Tera-huh?" He looked at GG pleadingly, his big eyes begging for help.

"It's one of those flying dinosaurs, everybody knows what they are," I remarked smugly.

"Alexis. Watch it." I thought she was warning me but when I saw her face, she was beaming at Harry whose eyes were, I couldn't believe it, changing colours. First they turned purple, then orange, and then light blue. Finally they settled on emerald green, just like mine. But that wasn't the only odd thing that happened. Slowly but surely, Harry's nose became longer and longer and his head became smaller. He was shrinking down, down, down until I couldn't see him because he was behind the counter. Suddenly, he swooped up to the ceiling and flew in circles around the light, making me feel dizzy. I realized I hadn't blinked since his eyes had started shifting and mine began to hurt. I rubbed them, in true cliché style, because I couldn't believe the message my optic nerves were generating to my brain. Harry had actually, in my own kitchen, morphed into a pterodactyl. Oh my gosh, he had just become a dinosaur from a billion years ago. Ohmygosh, ohmygosh!!! I started screaming with every square centimetre of air in my lungs and as I screamed out loud, I was yelling at myself inside to shut up and get a grip. But I couldn't. It was just too much all at once.

First I learn about the so called legend that is apparently true, then I find out the truth about my parents and now there was a giant bird dinosaur flapping through my house. I screeched all the way up my stairs and into my room. Once I got there I locked the door, the windows and all my cupboards and drawers. If the freaky morphing creature had already come in here to hide, it wouldn't be able to get out, and nothing could get in. I turned off the light and leapt into bed ensuring that if anything was under it, it wouldn't be able to grab my legs. Throwing the suffocating covers over myself and slamming my face into the pillow was my feeble attempt to help me rest and forget the goings-on downstairs. It took me a very, very long time to get to sleep.

THE SNAKE ENTRANCE

A knock on my door interrupted my flashback, but I ignored it thinking it must be GG. I lay my head back on my pillow and stayed as straight and as still as a pencil. Another knock and then a deep sigh when I didn't answer. I heard footsteps trudge slowly away and relaxed my muscles. They then tensed once again when I heard a quiet hiss to my left, near the door. As silently as I could I slipped out of bed on the right side and hid behind it. The hissing grew louder and louder. I raised my head over the bedside to see a small piece of rope come in under the door. A snake. It slithered slowly towards the bed, closer and closer it came, until it was out of my sight. Not knowing what to do, I sat on the floor, waiting for the creature to come out from under the bed on my side. It hissed again as it rose from the floor, raising its head to look at me. Could King Cobra's stand that tall? I didn't know but I stared at the thing in terror, its face getting wider and its body getting higher. Oh! It was Harry. He morphed back into himself and grimaced.

"Does it hurt when you...do it?" I asked, not wanting to offend him in case he got angry and turned into a bear or a lion.

"Yes, it does." He said simply. He thunked down on my bed and stared at me. After about a minute, I started to get self-conscious.

"What?"

"You are so ignorant about your destiny." My surprised look at his fortune cookie line must have surprised him too.

"What is that supposed to mean? Huh?" I asked defensively.

"You don't realize how much is riding on your shoulders. If you do not complete this mission to find the Ice Arrows, it'll be your fault if the world ends."

"Do you take me for an idiot? There are no such things as the Ice Arrows. The legend is just a little story you and GG made up in your heads. I don't know why, but I do know that it's all a trick!" On the last word, my voice kind of went really high, so it sounded more like I said "Treek!" This seemed to amuse Harry, even though I was in an almost-hysterical state. He smiled this amazing grin that could send shivers down any girl's spine, his face warm like the sun. That's when I noticed his hair. "Hey, did you dye your hair?"

He chuckled, "One minute you're yelling at me, the next you're staring at my hair! You are one confusing girl, Alexis Blake. Well, my hair changes colour each day, just like my eyes do when I shift. That's my name, by the way, Harry Shift." My disbelief was obviously covering my face because then he said, "What, you don't belief my hair changes colour, but you saw me morph into a dinosaur yesterday?"

"I just think it's weird that's all." He seemed hurt by this comment and we were silent for a while, "So why did you come in?" I blurted out.

"GG couldn't handle it. She wanted me to finish what she was saying yesterday. Did you realize that you slept for the whole afternoon and night? Anyway, I thought I'd carry on. You 'kay with that?" He looked at me, daring me to say no.

"On one condition."

"What?"

"Tell me about you first. How is it possible that you can morph into animals? It should be...well impossible." I wanted to know the secret behind how he had this magical power.

"Fine," he huffed, "I'll tell you all about me."

HARRY'S STORY

"I was born into a wealthy family, a really happy family. With two younger brothers and a sister I grew into being the one in charge. I liked it, being the boss all the time when Dad was at work. They would follow me around the house all day. I loved them very much. I was eight when Mum and Dad left me at home to babysit one day. They trusted me a great deal, you see. I decided we could have a picnic in the Nickel Forest, you know the one near the cliffs. Anyway, we went and had a whale of a time, playing tag and running about and eating until our stomachs were fit to burst. After we had all fallen on the floor completely stuffed, the second eldest, Jared had an idea. A very stupid idea. This is how the scene played out...

Jared: Hey, Harry. I bet I can go closer to the edge of the cliff than you.

Me: Uh, neither of us are going anywhere near the cliffs, mister. Let's go home and watch some T.V. and eat more!

(Other siblings cheer)

Jared: Just face it, you're a wuss.

Me: No I'm not. I just don't want to die! We are all going home.

Jared: I'm not. I'm staying right here.

(The other siblings know not to argue with me, so they step back)

Me: (turns around) Guys, you can go home, here's the key. Don't eat all the popcorn without us. (Back to Jared) Now you, sir, what did you say? You already know that when Mum and Dad are out I'm in charge and you have to do what you're told.

Jared: Not if what I'm being told to do is stupid.

Me: Jared, it's not stupid, it's for your own good. I don't think you want to fall off a cliff, do you?

(Silence)

Me: Okay then. (Turns back and starts to walk) Let's go home and watch cartoons, isn't your favorite show on today? Jared? Jared!

(Jared is running off into the forest towards the edge)

Me: Oh dear.

(Runs after him fast, but then hits head against a tree branch and falls over)

Me: Ow, that hurts.

(A scream is heard in the distance)

Me: Oh no, Jared.

Jared: Help! Help me, Harry!!!

Me: I'm coming Jared, hold on!

(Runs towards the edge, but sees nothing, thinks that Jared has fallen and leans over the edge)

Me: (whispered) Oh no, Jared, please be okay.

(Suddenly, Jared pops out behind me and scares me. I fall but manage to grab on to a branch)

Jared: Ahhh, Harry, hold on! You weren't supposed to fall! I was just going to scare you! Stay here, I'm going to go get help, I'll call Mum and Dad!!!

Me: No, Jared help me, I'm slipping!! Pull me up!

Jared: I have to go get help, I can't do it by myself, please just hold on!

(He runs away and leaves me by myself on the brink of falling off the edge.)

I was left alone for what felt like a long time, hanging on for dear life. Finally, I let go. Falling and falling to my death. I hit the ground and everything went black."

The little scene he had acted out had scared me half to death. How could a little boy be so cruel and not know it, leaving his big brother to just hang there.

"So, how are you alive? How are you standing in front of me? How the heck is all this possible?!"

"I wasn't finished. It turned out that I didn't fall as far as I had thought. I had actually landed on a ledge on the side of the cliff which happened to lead to a cave. I crawled inside and inspected myself. One thing about my family that you should know is that, physical pain doesn't affect us that much, but emotional pain really hurts us. I had three broken ribs, my elbow and leg were fractured and a broken nose. I'm not saying it didn't hurt, boy it did, but what hurt most was that my own brother had left me to fall. His intentions were good, and so I couldn't blame him, but it broke my heart."

"You still haven't answered my questions." I interrupted, starting to get annoyed.

He ignored me and went on, "I had nothing else to do but climb down. I figured it would be easier than climbing up and so I made my why down the ragged and jagged rocks of the cliff wall. It took me hours, maybe days, till I finally reached the bottom. I lost track of time. I hoped that maybe Mum and Dad would send out a search party but inside me, I knew they wouldn't."

"Why not?"

"Don't you know about the curse, the one about the valley?"

"No, tell me."

"Many people believe that there is a curse on the valley so that no one from either city can cross from one side to the other. My family believes it and so they knew that it would be hopeless to look for me, not just because I would be long gone, but also because they would come under the curse as well. Well, despite all of this I managed to survive."

"No duh."

An annoyed look shot in my direction. "Shut up and let me finish."

I shut up.

"As I was saying, until I was so rudely interrupted, I

made it down the valley. I lived there for at least eight weeks, eating discarded animal carcasses from Zoalan sacrifices, and drinking from a tiny stream that ran through the middle of the valley. Eventually the day came that I decided I had to climb back up. I wished with all my heart that I was a falcon so that I could just soar up. And it happened. I don't know how and I don't know why. Satisfied?"

"Yeah, kind of. So you have no idea how it happened, it just... did? I mean, how can you live with that humungous question hanging over you. I know I wouldn't be able to."

He didn't look up from inspecting his finger nails, "Well, I guess I don't really care. I mean, if you could do anything you wanted and be anything you wanted, would you really care where that power came from. I prefer not to question it."

"I guess you're right, but wouldn't you want to thank whoever gave it to you?"

"Sometimes I do, under my breath."

We stayed there for a while, pondering these thoughts, until I remembered the actual, original reason why he was in my room.

"So what else did you want to tell me about this story of yours? You know, you said that GG wanted you to finish off what she was saying last night."

"Oh yeah, right." He reached into his jacket pocket and pulled out a small, black, leather book with an embossed picture of fire on the front. It was filled to the brim with notes and pages overflowing with words. It was beautiful, the perfect little diary. It looked so old it could have been my- oh! my grandfather's.

"So is this it, my grandfather's diary of his adventure?" I muttered as I inspected it for any hidden cameras. I opened it at the table of contents. It looked something like this:

The Journey: threats and their habitats:

- The Nowhere District
- The Vicious Volcano
- Leopard Lizards
- Hungry Lava
- The Slanting Ship
- Minty Mourners
- The Ticker
- The Doomful Desert
- The Scorcher
- Fox Flies
- Bolts
- Batteries
- The Carnivorous Cave with Stabbing Stalactites and Stinging Stalagmites

"Wow, whoever wrote this really liked alliteration! My grandfather was crazy, just as I suspected." A thought then struck me, "how do you know GG, Harry?"

Harry surprised by the question, answered in a quick sentence, "I saved her when her house was burning down." And that was that.

I continued to inspect the book, reading different little segments. The material that they were using for this con was quite spectacular. I mean, it must've taken months to make up these different things. I still just didn't understand why they were conning me.

"Read the section on The Hungry Lava," Harry ordered me. I had forgotten he was there and was quite taken aback when he broke the silence. I obeyed and opened the book to the correct page. Harry nodded as I read aloud.

"At the bottom of the vicious volcano heat springs up every so often, that creates the smokiest of ash clouds. Far beneath these grey pillows is an angry monster, a hungry monster. The Hungry Lava. As a seeker climbs down the rocky edges of the inner-mountain, the red liquid heat laps at their heels, burning any normal person. But if a fire demon ever reached this point in the adventure, they would only feel warm water at their ankles. But they still must be wary of their footing because the man-eating liquid will show no mercy." I recited out of the book, then looking at Harry questioningly, "So?"

FLYING FIRE

Instead of answering he walked over to the fireplace and placed three logs in it, then lit them. It took a while to start up but after about five minutes there was a roaring fire, burning bright. I joined him, sitting cross legged by the fire. I stared into it, conjuring pictures in my mind. I could see a vibrant lion roaring, a phoenix flapping its wings and dancing under the sun. I loved looking into fires, they danced before me. They never burned my eyes, I could look at them all day.

"Your eyes..." Harry mumbled.

"What about my eyes?" I quickly retorted. If he wanted to compliment me I would have clipped him right in the chin. But the moment was lost as I was yet again mesmerized by the flame's exuberant dancing.

"Touch the fire, Alexis. Go on, you know you want to." He suddenly ordered.

"Why would I do that, I'm not an idiot," I murmured, transfixed as if I were hypnotised, "It would burn me."

"Not you, anyone else but you. You are a fire

demon." The last two words were whispered into my ear like they were the most important words ever told.

With my eyes glazed over, I slowly raised my hands towards the scorching heat. It grew warmer and warmer until I was sure that my hands were going to burn. But as I reached forward, I didn't feel the slightest pain, just the warm comfort you feel after you've been cold for a long, long time. I looked down to see that my hands were in the middle of the flames and were glowing but otherwise not affected. As I slowly turned my palms upwards, I felt a surge of power rush through me. Was he actually telling the truth? Did I actually have power over fire?

"No way," I breathed, "this is incredible, how is this possible?"

"Grace and I have been telling you how for the last two days, but you haven't been listening?" he teased with a hint of humour.

I raised a hand up, most of the fire just resting on my palm. This was amazing. I then decided to do an experiment. Picturing in my mind the night before when Harry had turned into a dinosaur, I used my other hand to shape my fire. Using my imagination, the fire danced in a way so that it played out the scene. Not only was I amazed, but so was Harry.

"I wonder if I could…" I stood up slowly, holding the flames in my hands. Walking carefully so that it wouldn't fall, I staggered towards the window.

"Hey Harry, could you open this for me, my hands are kinda full."

"Sure." He lifted the window frame all the way to the

top. "What are you going to do?"

"I'm going to fly."

"You're going to what?!"

"Wait and see." I leant out of the window, putting the fire into one hand so that I could hold on to the window frame with the other. With my fire hand to my mouth, I blew the magnificent flames into the sunny day outside. It came out in a sort of sheet, like red paper, but surprisingly solid. I tested it for sturdiness and lifted one foot out of the window.

"Woah, what are you doing? This is too new to you, you don't know how to use it properly yet, how can you be sure you're ready?"

"Trust me, I know."

"Why should I trust you?"

I didn't answer, but instead I stepped from the window on to the fire plank. My stomach was spinning about like a hurricane from anxiety and excitement. As I rested both feet on the fire I thought, *This is it, I have finally found out why I'm alive, this is what I was born to do* and I let go of the window frame. At first I was a bit wobbly but when I concentrated on my balance I was fine and steady. I moved the board around in a circle. Woah!

"Dude, it's just like a surf board!" Harry yelled at me. I was already half way across the field. The air was flying past my face as I went faster and faster, past the forest behind the field and over the meadows. I swerved away from the cliffs and headed into town. It was amazing being so high above everyone else, like riding in a helicopter but without the space restriction. I spread my arms out and swooped in a circle like a bird of prey. Kind of like a pterodactyl. I dove into the middle of the town square and did a round of the shops. It was too early for them to be open, so I had the place to myself. I stopped in front of the grocer's and stole an apple from out front. I felt so free and alive, no one stopping me from doing what I wanted. No Lola shouting at me to drop and do one hundred. Eventually I decided it would be best to head back and get everything sorted out. I could come surfing again later. As I passed back over the field I heard a small voice yelling my name from beneath me. I looked down to see who was shouting at me. It was GG. My concentration was shattered and I fell down and down.

UNDERSTANDING FIRE POWER

It turned out that I wasn't that far up because I didn't pass out when I hit the ground. The fire was lost in the wind, blown away because I wasn't keeping it alive. Oh well.. I sat up and looked at my surroundings. GG was rushing towards me out of breath. Harry had shifted into a falcon and came swooping down.

"Oh sweetie, are you okay? You were amazing. Who knew your power was so strong? You just have to remember to concentrate next time, okay."

My skin burned, "FYI, GG you were the one who made me lose my focus so why don't you just shut-"

"Let's get pie for breakfast; Lola saw some come out of the oven fresh this morning." Harry interrupted. Bernie was the town's baker, well he wasn't really a baker, and he didn't own a shop or anything. He just liked to cook and so sometimes people would drop in and pick up something he had made.

The interruption dissipated my anger and so I was calmer as GG, Harry and I slowly meandered back to the house, not looking at each other. Harry, finally, decided to break the ice.

"Your boarding was awesome. I didn't know you could do that. Did you, Grace?"

GG looked up as if she hadn't been listening, "Hm? What did you say?"

"Alexis's boarding. Did you know that she could do that?"

"Oh yeah sure. She does have power over fire, sweetie." She muttered quietly.

"One thing I don't understand is how I haven't been able to do these things before. I mean, when I was six, I burnt my hand trying to light the fire myself."

"It's probably because you only just learnt about your powers. You didn't know you had them before so you didn't use them, you didn't focus on them. Now that you believe, you are able." She answered solemnly, very deep.

"Hm," I digested this response because there wasn't any other explanation I could think of. Then, out of the blue, I made a big decision. I was going to believe them. So, it didn't matter if this was all a big con, if there was no such thing as the Leopard Lizards or Fox Flies. Besides, I had nothing to lose.

When we eventually got back to the house, Harry and I went up to my room to retrieve, the book so that all three of us could discuss it over pie.

"I'll go see Bernie and get the pies, what type would ya like?"

"Don't care, whatever he's got." I mumbled as I hurried in to find the diary. Harry walked close behind me, then towards the window. "Well, aren't ya going to go get them?"

"Yeah, I'm going."

"Well, the door is that way." I motioned towards the door.

"Flying is faster." Before I could say anything else, the wind from outside started blowing around him, turning him into a mini whirl wind. His morphing cycle began, lengthening his arms to make giant wings. But then it all stopped. He stood there with wings instead arms.

"Um, is that it?"

"Yeah, what's the point in going through the pain of shifting into a different creature completely, when I can just grow wings."

This seemed fair, so I nodded and continued to hunt between the sheets for the book. Where was it? Oh, beneath my pillow where I had left it. I jumped when I heard a loud *thunk* coming from the window. Harry was flapping away outside and had closed the window by kicking it down with his foot. I used the banister to slide down the stairs landing in the dent I had made over the years. It was part of my daily routine. The kitchen door was open so I went straight in, expecting to see GG waiting for me. Well I was right about that, but I really didn't expect Lola to be sitting opposite to her chatting away like her best buddy. I coughed loudly so that they would know I was there and made my way towards the fridge. Lola's conversation screeched to halt as I walked past her.

"Alexis."

"Hm?"

"I am glad to hear that you have come to your senses. You are going, are you not?" Lola always got straight to the point.

"You knew about this?" I yelled, pointing my finger at her accusingly.

"I knew about your destiny, yes. I did not know where your grandmother was, though, so I have committed no crime. When your parents disappeared I swore an oath that I would not tell you about your future until a next of kin was found."

"Oh." I said, embarrassed. She got down from her stool and came over to me. "You must do this, Alexis," putting her hands on my shoulders. "It is what you were born to do." Then she walked out of the front door.

PIE AND AN ACCIDENT

Harry came in about five minutes later in normal human form, with three pieces of pie. Chocolate for me, lemon sherbet for GG and blueberry cheesecake for himself. We tucked in and didn't stop or talk until we were all finished. GG cleared the table and washed up. Harry and I continued our conversation from before.

"So, do you feel that you need more training? With your fire power, I mean."

"Um, I think I can learn. What I'm most worried about is this whole 'adventure' that you guys are talking about. Like, is it going to be proper-Indiana-Jones-adventure or holiday-in-lots-of-different-places-around-the-world-adventure. "

"More like an every-minute-you're-scared-for-your-life-because-its-always-in-danger-adventure." GG shouted over the sound of the tap water, not looking up from her important washing up. Well, that sure made me feel better about my decision. I raised my eyebrows at the back of her head.

"Well, urm, thank you for that valuable information, I will cherish it every step of the journey."

"Sarcasm is not going to get you anywhere, honey." She replied.

"Do you want to practice some stuff now?" Harry chimed in, ignoring GG's comment.

"Sure. Let's go back up to my room." We ran up the stairs and into my room. Slightly out of breath, I dropped down next to the ever roaring fire. As soon as my bum touched the floor, the flames jumped, making me jump also. It had become bigger because I was sitting next to it. Cool. As in awesome-cool, because it was definitely nothing but hot now that the red tongues were so big.

"So," I said as I stared at the fire, "How shall we start?"

"I don't know, you're the one with all the power over this stuff," he motioned to the fire with the hand he wasn't leaning on. As I stared into the fire, I had an epiphany. I wondered if I could fight with this stuff. Maybe throw fire balls like in those cartoons that guys are always reading and watching. I decided to try it. I got up from my seat on the floor, marched over to the window and opened it once again. I bent down to collect a small amount of orange and red. Holding it carefully in the palm of my hand, I walked slowly to the far end of the room facing the window, hoping that it would make it that far. I formed it into a ball shape with my hands. And then spinning the ball of fire I lurched forward. At first, I thought it would make it, but my hopes were crushed when it fell short of the window and my bed went up in flames. There was a slight panic while Harry ran out of the room to find the hall fire extinguisher and I tried to calm it down by blowing and picking bits up and putting them back into the fireplace. He burst through the door and sprayed the white powdery stuff all over my bed. Great! The sofa is not the most comfortable sleeping accommodation. He also blew out the fire place. He was so cleaning that mess up.

"Why don't you just change into a polar bear and stomp it out?" I asked, only half serious.

"There is something you should understand. It really does hurt when I change, so I don't like to do it that often, so stop bugging me about it, okay," he snarled as he inspected the damage, not even looking at me. "You were the one who asked me if it hurts in the first place."

"Okay, I'm sorry."

We met GG on the stairs. She had heard the commotion and was running up to see what the fuss was about. Harry gave me a 'let's not tell her until she finds out' look. I nodded.

"I fell over into the fire, I screamed because I forgot about my powers. It was pretty funny actually." I smiled and Harry chuckled along awkwardly. Sometimes I scare myself by how well I can lie. Well, if it gets me out of trouble, hey. Harry stared at me like I was some sort of goddess. The Goddess of Pretending. I know, I know. Please, no pictures!

"Well, don't do it again, you almost gave me a heart attack." Even if it had happened, how would I have prevented it? Ugh, adults!

So, that night, around the dinner table, we planned the journey. We would leave in three days time for the

Hidden Door which leads to the Nowhere District where the adventure would start. According to Grandpa's book, the Nowhere District is just a gigantic vast space of nothing but flowers, miles and miles of flowers. And the best part is they talk. Well they don't exactly talk, they speak in song. They are called Singers, duh. But the weirdest part about them, is that they can read your thoughts. So best not think of them as wierd, because they might start screaming at you in opera. I was still not completely sure about all this fantasy, but then again, I had been flying on a surfboard made out of fire, so who was I to doubt them. Afterwards, I read almost the whole of Grandpa's diary. He must have been a pretty funny guy. There were so many side notes of things he would have liked GG to see and vivid descriptions of what he saw. For example, according to his eyes, the Vicious Volcano looked like an inside-out belly button. Yuck, but funny.

Looking through it, I believed more and more. Since I was on the lumpy sofa for the night (whoops!) I couldn't sleep at all. In the middle of the night, Mr Macho came in to see if I was okay.

"I'm fine, although I think I would sleep better if I hadn't set my bed on fire."

"You're making it sound like it was my fault. Anyway I was just checking to see if you were okay."

"Yeah, you said that already." I pointed out.

"Oh." He was acting strangely and I didn't know exactly what to do. I mean I had only met the dude the day before, and now he was standing next to me in the middle of the night. What was I supposed to say?

"Um, no offense, but is that it? I mean, you come looking for at me at," I checked my watch, "2:30 in the morning just to check on me. Is everything okay?"

"Well, you're only thirteen. And this trip is going to be dangerous. I thought you might be… ya know… scared."

"I've got nothing to lose. "

"Me neither." He whispered quietly, a thick sadness in his voice.

GG!

Waking up on leaving day was like waking up on Christmas Day. I was so excited. I started packing up my stuff even though I had hardly any idea what I needed.

"You're not going to need all that stuff." Harry said, as if reading my mind.

"Whaddya mean?"

"Look, do you really think we're going to be able to hold on to these things?" He came and knelt next to me, taking out different bits and bobs I had packed. "Do you really need books? I mean it's not like you're going to have time to read, with all the running around and stuff."

"Yeah, I guess." I started unpacking.

"When do you suppose we leave?"

"Soonish, I guess." I really had no idea. How was I supposed to know when we were going to start on this life threatening journey? We didn't speak as I unpacked. Eventually my pack contained a bottle of sunscreen, Grandpa's book, some clothes and a couple of snacks. Maybe a few more than a couple. As I reached down to pick up more food, Harry picked up more clothes.

"I'm not that girly, I don't mind wearing dirty clothes, ya know." I looked at Harry; my brain was saying 'Sexist!!!'.

"I don't think two or three outfits is enough for almost a year, girly or not." My jaw dropped, if my life were a cartoon, it would have touched the floor.

"A year?!" As I said this I moved my lower jaw around to click it back into place, so it sounded kind of weird.

"Less if you run fast." With that, he left. His cheeky grin always took me by surprise.

It's not that I liked him. It was just that he was so... not wanting to use a cliché but, well, yummy.

I ran out of the door behind him. "What do you mean 'a year'?" I yelled after him. He didn't answer, of course. I ran to GG's room to ask her. When I signed up for this, I didn't know it was going to take that long!

I barged into the room, steaming like a lobster "GG, what the heck? A year? Nobody told me this, I mean I knew it took Grandpa a long time but, ya know, can't Harry just turn into an airplane and fly there? GG, get out of bed! This is serious!" I went to shake her awake but the lumps were just sheets. The awkwardness you feel when you realize you've been screaming at an empty bed in the middle of a rant is overwhelming. I knocked on the door of the bathroom, quietly. "Grandma, are you in there?" My face was bright red with anger and embarrassment.

"Yes, Alexis." It was obvious from her voice that she

was trying to suppress giggles. She had probably heard the whole thing.

"Could you come out, please?" On the word, 'come' my voice cracked and went higher. I felt so stupid.

"Hold on, let me just fix up." Now I know I'm not a very girly girl, but it shouldn't take half an hour for *anyone* to 'just fix up'. I was so bored and getting impatient, so I started to snoop. My parents disappeared, I only learnt army morals. The guest room wasn't that big, so I managed to look around the whole place. I just wanted to make absolutely sure that this wasn't a con. My last stop of the room was at the night stand. And, woah, did I get a shock there. When I looked in the desk drawer I found the weirdest thing I've ever seen in an old woman's… well, anything. I didn't even know what it was. It was like a big battery stuck to the side of the drawer. Could it be a-

"Alexis," she sounded worried, so maybe she suspected that I'd found what she was hiding. "Sweetie, what are you doing?"

"Nothing, I just knocked into something, its fine." I lied. I managed to sit on the end of her bed and pretend to have been there for the whole time.

She came out in her robe with her toothbrush in her hand.

"What did you need, honey?" She moved to stand in front of the desk. Thankfully, she didn't suspect that I'd been looking. Ugh, I just wanted to get out of there and tell Harry. I stood up and shimmied towards the exit.

"See ya."

"What happened?" Harry was sitting at the counter eating a chocolate sundae. He probably read the disgusted expression on my face

"Um, it's hard to explain." I sat down, took a spoon out of the drawer and started picking at his cream. He pulled away immediately, a fake kiddy face that said 'mine'. Then he relaxed, smiling and put the sundae in between us.

"I will tell you if I get lost." He looked at me and stared all serious, even though we both knew he just wanted to know. I really needed to tell, though, so explained what I saw.

"It had a little green flashing light on it, to signify it was on or something. Or activated. This is probably just me overreacting so it could just be nothing but… well, I've seen enough spy movies to think that kinda looked like a, ya know, a bug."

He chuckled nervously, "Who would bug Grace?" as soon as he finished saying it his face sunk with a knowing expression. "I know who."

"Who?"

He sighed, "Zacheri Smoke." His voice was deeper than I had ever heard it. I expected it to have broken already, but it seemed that it was in the process because sometimes it sounded different. I forgot about the words he said and just pondered about his tone. I didn't want to admit it myself but I too had the same fear when I first saw it.

"Should we dispose of it?"

He cocked an eyebrow at me. I realized what I had said sounded like I was a spy-wannabe. I continued, ignoring his expression. "GG makes diary logs using her recorder instead of writing entries. That is probably why he placed it there, unless he's just lucky." Then it hit me. If Zacheri Smoke had been listening in on her diary entries, then he would know we were going. He was going to try and get rid of us like he got rid of my parents.

"Remind me again, what his deal is?"

He shuffled his bum to get more comfy. This was going to be a long talk.

"Why don't you just read it in the book?" He sighed.

"Fine." I pulled it out from my back jean's pocket.

"Could you read it out loud?"

"Sure, but it's not very good writing, not to diss Grandpa or anything." I started reading.

"'Kay, here we go. "He is also trying to find the three Arrows, not to bring back the Ice Empress, but to destroy her. He and his family were related to Vola, the King's advisor, who blamed the Ice Empress for destroying the monarchy and so destroying his world of power and authority. Vola's descendants have always hated those who thought the Ice Empress was good, so much so that they even started a genocide in Zoal against her supporters. Zacheri Smoke has childish features but a big, strong body, almost eight feet tall. He acts as if everything is a game. In his childhood, he was hit by an electric sky train at full speed, crushing him on the tracks. He survived through magic and decided that he was brought back

to life to complete the mission of destroying the Ice Arrows. He was left with many scars all over his body and one long scar right through his bald, shiny head. A long line where his skin had split open. When he was hit, electricity engulfed him and left him with supernatural power over it. He can shoot Bolts and can harness any electricity around him to fight."
Wow, this dude is scarred. Literally and figuratively." I hardly took a breath through the whole speech. I was scared for GG and for everyone else. I glanced at Harry, to see what he was thinking.

"I met him once." His face was a cross between wistful and full of pain, as if he was reliving a terrible memory. I leaned closer. "You haven't read the bit about his Bat-eries."

"His huh?"

"Miniature, electric bats surround the dark Zacheri Smoke, sort of like his henchmen. They send little shockwaves of insanity through the brain of his enemies that only last for about ten seconds. Then they have to recharge for 5 minutes. Can be fatal to those who don't believe in the impossible. A vivid imagination can overpower a bat-ery if one chooses the right moment." He sounded as if he was quoting from someone, but I didn't bother to ask.

A noise came from upstairs. Our faces were frozen with fear. A scream. We both heard it and at the exact same moment, we leapt from our chairs and ran. Taking two steps at a time, racing down the hall, kicking down the door of GG's bedroom but it was all for nothing. She was gone. Zacheri had taken her.

We searched the streets, neighbours' houses and every

shop in town. We (well, I, Harry was afraid) even peeked over the cliffs. We checked everywhere, but we couldn't find her. I had never shed a tear in my life but I could feel the dust prickling my eyes. I rubbed them, with my back turned to Harry so that he wouldn't think I was crying. When I turned back, it was obvious he had no problem crying in front of people. He was sitting on a bench, his head in his hands. What was I supposed to do? This had never happened to me before. I'd never been in this sort of situation. I edged closer, trying to seem casual. I sat down next to him, glancing in his direction, a stupid part inside of me angry at *him* because I was the one who had *to* comfort and not the one to *be* comforted. I mean, she was my grandmother. Even though I hadn't known her long.

"She was like a mom to me, ever since I fell from the cliff. After I saved her from her burning house she took me in. My parents didn't want me anymore because of the curse." Harry blurted out. I instantly felt guilty. That explained a lot.

We stayed there for a long time. Eventually Harry stopped crying and just sat and stared at the ground, his depressed expression looking like it was permanently attached to his face. Suddenly, a burning rage grew in me that I should have had all long.

"I'm going to kill Zacheri Smoke."

"We'll do it together." The defiance in his tone made my heart rise so high it was in my mouth. We ran back to the house, picked up our stuff and left for the Nowhere District.

BUSY ROADS AND BUSY RATS

The Hidden Door matched its name perfectly; it was such a nightmare to find. Grandpa had written a series of riddles to guide us to it. He wrote it in a sort of code, which we had to decipher. He wasn't the greatest when it came to inventing riddles.

The first one said 'Go west at the gate of sweet smelling serenity. It's displayed but not for sale'. That must be Bernie's house. His family has been baking for ages. You could call it a family business although you'd be wrong because it's all free. We went west past his little blue cottage and stopped to read the next clue. It felt so cheesy, like we were on a kiddy's treasure hunt, following riddles for little chocolate prizes. If only we were dressed in Easter Bunny costumes.

Then it started getting tricky. There was a fork in the road next to Bernie's house and the clue didn't tell us which road to go down. We realized that one of the roads was only recently built so Grandpa's directions were a bit hard to follow. "A man made emptiness, although not made of man, in the midst of man's rush to reach his destination", I shouted over the loud traffic. We eventually figured that we had to go down a manhole in the middle of the original left fork road. Great. It was rush hour. And when it's rush hour in this town, you don't cross the road unless you have a death wish.

"Okay, I have a plan. You turn into a raccoon, get hit and become road kill. The driver will stop so I can cross that lane. That's all I got so far." I was only half serious. He was still depressed and upset so he ignored my suggestion. We watched hundreds of cars go by, feeling more hopeless with every second. "So what do you suggest?"

"I say we wait until rush hour is over and all the cars have gone."

"Nah, let's just go now." Not waiting for his answer, I jumped into the middle of the traffic. It was sort of like a ballet, imagine me dodging vehicles, my movements matched the rhythm of a Strauss Waltz. Da dadadada, di di, di di, da dadadada, di di, di di. Right foot, left foot, jump over a motorbike; I was having a great time. All those hours on the dreaded ropes course paid off. As I looked back in mid split jump over a car, I saw Harry's expression. It was hilarious. His mouth was in a tight 'O' shape and his eye balls were bulging. I let out a cackle as I landed on the manhole after my elegant leap. I turned to face him and gave a little curtsy. I wasn't watching the cars at that point and Harry quickly unfroze.

"'Lexis, look out for the-"Something very hard and heavy hit my side. It knocked me to the ground as it screeched to a halt. At least it hadn't slammed into me at full speed. The screeching tires rang in my ears as loads of cars stopped and honked their horns in frustration at the hold up. After a few minutes it didn't hurt so much so I stood up and waved at all the honking road ragers. It would just leave a nasty bruise. Since the traffic had come to a halt, Harry, calm and collected as usual, strode to my side. He knelt down and with his manly muscles lifted the manhole cover. I gave one last menacing wave to the drivers, some of whom had started to get out of their cars, and swiftly lowered myself down. When I got to eye level with Harry, he was wearing a very cheeky grin.

"Your plan worked, except you were almost the road kill."

"Oh, ha ha." I said sarcastically.

I dropped from the ladder into water. "Oh, ew. This better be just a storm drain."

"It is," he pointed to a printed sign next to the ladder, "so what's the next clue, Watson?"

"Huh?"

"'Heard of Sherlock Holmes?"

"Duh." Even though I had no idea what he was talking about.

"You're Watson, the sidekick." I nodded dumbly and read the next riddle.

"'Follow the ginger brick tunnel, to your heart's desire. It may not smell as it sounds.'" I guessed that this meant that the door was at the end of the tunnel. But we had one problem, the tunnel wasn't ginger, it was red. "Do ya think my grandpa was colour blind, possibly?"

"No, he wasn't. There's a tunnel down there that seems to be a different shade." I looked to where he was pointing and, sure enough, the tunnel was a strange shade of orange like the chief policeman's hair. He let me stroke it once and I decided never to touch a bald man's gelled-up wig ever again. I waded to the grating that was the entrance to the tunnel and broke the lock with the crowbar I just happened to have in my bag.

"I didn't see you pack that." He said like an over controlling mother. I didn't tell him about it because I knew he wouldn't let me take it. I didn't respond.

What, a girl on the run can't have a weapon? I felt really tough as I smashed that lock to bits. Harry did the honours of opening the grate but then pointed out something else that I hadn't noticed. It was because I was much shorter than him. He pointed up to a sign that said 'sewage canal'. Oh, no. Please, no!

He pushed me aside. I guess he was trying to show his manliness by stepping into the claustrophobic faeces-filled passageway first. While he was being manly, I was busy being squeamish.

"There is no way I am going in there."

"Come on, don't be so girly."

"Okay first of all that is sexist and second of all, dude the tunnel is full of…you know…pooh." Something about just saying the word made me feel dirty.

"Oh look, there's a rat floating on a piece of poop, how cute."

I glared at him.

"Look, maybe you're just not up for this whole thing. I mean, how could somebody who is afraid of getting a little dirty be in a life or death situation almost all the time."

"We are in a life/death situation if we hang around in excrement! Ever heard of cholera!" I screamed at him. I can get a bit stubborn sometimes. I'm not saying I'm scared, but I just can't stand rodents. You're probably thinking 'Oh, what about hamsters and guinea pigs, they're adorable.' Well, I don't think so.

"Come on, girl it's not like we're going to be eating it and it doesn't even come up to my knees."

"*Your* knees!"

"If you are not coming, then I'm going. See ya."

Oh no, no way was he going to leave me alone with rats. I raised my leg to get in through the small entrance that Harry had smoothly slid through. I gripped on to the side wall handle and pulled the other leg up. To get down to the floor, I had to jump. At least the sneakers I was wearing weren't new.

"Come on, midget!" Harry yelled from halfway down the tunnel. Even though I didn't appreciate the short joke (I was average height, he was the giant) I felt a little bit more confident and finally slipped from the edge. Plop! I landed with a thud, but safe. I grinned, a rush of pride ran through me, which was my first mistake. My second mistake was not realizing that my shoes were untied. One step and splat, right on to something squishy and warm. A rat. A scream escaped from my lips and I heard Harry's big footsteps come running. It seemed like the rat was screaming too, because a high pitched squeal was coming from under me. I had fallen pretty hard and hurt my knee so I wasn't sure if I could get up myself.

"Oh my gosh, Harry help me! There's a rat, there's a rat!" A sting came from my belly, then another and another. It was trying to dig its way through me; it was probably drowning, and let me tell ya I didn't care. Out of shear horror and disgust, I had kept my head out of the horrible smelling liquid; you could hardly call it water.

He laughed when he saw my dilemma. He couldn't stop. I wanted to swipe his feet out from under him, but I was too busy screaming my head off. He calmed down but was still giggling.

"Just get up, fool." He half laughed, half ordered. He extended a hand and I took it, lifting me to my feet in one swift motion. Boy, he was strong. After a moment of cleaning myself up (using our whole supply of tissues) we continued walking down the muddy lane. As we waded I checked out the wounds inflicted by the squished and drowning rat. It had ripped open my shirt, but only enough to reveal my belly button so I wasn't that fussed. There were some small cuts from his claws, but nothing a plaster couldn't fix. It had really hurt though, but I could tell that Harry thought I was a big baby, screaming about a rat. Who wouldn't scream if a large rodent was clawing at their skin? Harry would probably say that he was doing it in self-defence, but it just goes to show that rats are definitely not pacifists.

"One thing still confuses me." Harry spoke up out of

the blue.

"What?"

"Well, if the door is at the end of this tunnel, then any sewage worker guy could find it. It's not very hidden." I hadn't thought of that.

"Well the lock seemed kind of rusty. Maybe nobody's chosen to come down here because they don't have the key. One of those what-dya-call-ems wouldn't risk their jobs out of pure curiosity. I mean, wouldn't they have to pay if they broke the lock?"

"Hm." That was the end of that discussion.

After a while I started to get impatient, asking Harry every now and then to the read the directions again (there was no way I was taking my eyes off the ground after the rat incident). When I asked him to read it a fourth time, he gave up. He told me to occupy myself some other way, but how was I supposed to do that when my eyes were glued to the floor. I was angry now and created a list in my head of all the horrible things I could do to Harry for being a jerk.

"I like your hair." Well that was random. I was taken aback by his sudden compliment and I didn't know how to respond.

"Uh…thanks." I managed, choking on my words. I didn't know what anyone could see in short, scraggly black hair. Lola had said that black was good; you wouldn't be able to see all the mud. I used to have long hair which Lola taught me to put up in a tight bun every morning, but when I got sick of it I just chopped it off with a pair of scissors. Lola didn't even notice it was gone until I went up the stairs; she looked after me and nearly knocked the sofa over trying to get to me and my hair. I told this story to Harry and it made him grin. "Well, my hair changes colour." I still couldn't believe that. It was just so weird. Then I remembered that I was following around a boy who could change into any animal he wanted. I felt a little light bulb turn on over my head.

"Hey, Harry?"

"Yeah."

"Can you morph into a rat and tell them to keep to the sides? They keep trying to eat my laces."

"Uh," he let out a confused smile, "I guess." He motioned for me to squat down, then he put his foot into my hand. "Aw, yuck! Dude, remember what you've been walking in."

"It's the same stuff that's all over your clothes and body." I let out a sigh.

He started to shake violently. It was even weirder than usual to watch him so close up. He shrank in my hand. Harry was sitting on my hand, rat size and rat like. He started to squeak, not at me but in the direction of a group of rats in the middle of the path. It was actually kinda cute because they responded to him in chorus. They were like drones, but with really high pitched voices and they were talking in their native tongue. His little body turned back to me.

"Done." Woah, it was Harry speaking, but like a six year old girl. I was trying really hard not to burst out laughing. I failed.

"AHAHHAHAHAHHAHAHAHAHA." I actually started crying, as in laughing crying, not upset crying. I never cry. Ever.

"Oh, shut up." Harry squealed. Another round of laughs burst out of me and I couldn't stop, I almost fell over. He jumped off my hand and made a wee splash in the water, spraying my face as I was doubled up laughing. That sure shut me up.

"Hey dude, that went in my mouth! Aw, disgusting, man!!" I yelled at him. He was doggy paddling away through the brown slush, as if in a ratty huff. I started howling again. A sulking fourteen year old boy who had morphed into a rat with a six year old girl's voice, *doggy paddling!* It was just too much. "I'll stop laughing if you turn back!" I chortled. I don't usually use the word 'chortle' but it definitely fits what I did.

He tried to make his voice sound deeper but it only made it sound like a kid with a really sore throat, "'Felt like swimming, it's easier."

Eventually the hysterical chortles turned into a quiet giggle. Only then did I realize, other than the squeaking of rats and the splashing of Harry's little paws, how quiet it was. Splish, splosh, splish, splosh, as he tried to master crawl with an overgrown mouse's body. It was funny to watch at first, but soon the novelty wore off. As we sauntered and swam deeper and deeper into the tunnel, I became accustomed to the smell. But the more I got used it, the more impatient I got.

"Do you reckon we're almost there?

"Yes. There." His tiny paw pointed forward. And

there I saw it. Not the door, but a fork in the pathway.

SPLIT UP

"Okay, two directions, one leading to who knows where, the other leading to 'our heart's desire'. The problem is we don't know which one is which. Check the book again for anything your daddy pops may have said that we missed." Harry was doing the swimming equivalent of pacing, back and forth in front of me, while I stood stock still, my eyes going mad looking from one path to the other, both menacingly dark and mysterious.

"You know you could probably pace better if you were human." I didn't know I was saying the words. I was concentrating so hard on the question buzzing in my head that I didn't even hear his response. I pulled the book out of my pocket and held it out towards him. I was too busy to read it. He grew taller and taller next to me, and then finally snatched the book out of my hand. My face shot him an evil glare and then went back to staring at our options. I did notice something though. Was Harry hairier than usual? I turned back and to my horror, he was still a rat, but his normal human size. I let out a small squeak, which was ironic since the thing I was afraid of had squeakish down as one his many fluent languages. He stood in a fashion model pose, his front legs crossed across his chest, slightly leaning back with most of his weight on one back leg. I swore at him so harshly that he grimaced.

"Dude, What the heck? It was just a joke." He smiled at me, hoping I'd see his side and forgive.

Not going to happen, "You. Know. I. Hate. RATS!" I yelled rats so loud that it echoed down both hallways. He was obviously momentarily surprised by my outburst, but then he just went on giggling. "Read the friggin' book, will ya." I growled.

"Okay, here we go. Oh yeah we missed a part of the riddle. "Follow the ginger brick tunnel, to your heart's desire. It may not smell as it sounds. When you reach a pinnacle decision, wait for your instinct."

"So I guess this is the pinnacle decision." I pointed out the obvious.

"I'm guessing we have to 'wait for your instinct' to kick in?"

"Yeah, I suppose." To occupy myself, I walked over to the wall and started making scratches with the pen knife Lola had given me. I drew a picture of two dark alleys and a whole bunch of little balls running down it. The balls were supposed to be rats, but I'm not really the artistic sort. We waited for the wind to blow in my Grandfather's name, but it never came.

"I think we have to choose," I decided, "I'll go this way, you go that way." I didn't get a chance to take a step before Harry jumped in front of me.

"Your grandmother told me to stay near you at all costs. I don't break promises." Taking a walkie talkie he had strapped to the side of his bag and giving it to him, I walked on.

"See ya."

Splitting up wasn't actually the perfect idea. As I walked further and further down the passage-way it got really dark and the air was getting thinner. Every now and then, I had to brush off spider's webs I stumbled through. It seemed that it was much the same for Harry too.

"Alexis, are you there?" the rustling noise of the walkie-talkie made me jump. "Can you hear me?" He sounded kind of scared; I believe men shouldn't show fear.

"I'm here, over."

"There are so many spider webs and it's so freakin' dark. And you're the one with the flash light." He grumbled, I gave a smug look to the wall, in the direction of where I thought he'd be. I switched it on and looked around my area. There were no rats anymore, so that was a bonus. I grew more confident and sped up my pace since I could see where I was going. After a while, I contacted Harry.

"How's it going, over?"

"Same as before. Webs and water and rats."

"Rats, really? I don't have any on this side. Over." I skidded to a halt. If I didn't have rats on my side, I must have a dead end, which meant that the door was on my side.

"Harry, the door is on my side, turn back, over." I yelled excitedly when I figured it out.

He didn't say anything but pressed the button so that

I could hear the splash of his feet running in the sewage. I ran towards the place where we had parted company.

"Get on my back, now." He leant down to give me a piggy back. I jumped on and immediately he morphed into something different. I couldn't see what he was, but he was very fast. We were in pitch blackness when I heard a voice.

"The Light." It was deep and majestic, like I imagined a big cat to sound. Harry must have turned into a cheetah or something. I switched on the flash light and held it in front of us. His beautiful gold and dotted black coat shimmered in the light. His eyes gleamed like diamonds. He was gorgeous and I was bewitched. As the pounding slowed down, I looked up to see the door right in front of us. Remembering the spell Grandpa had written in order to open the door, I screamed, "Mag too le sefa!" The entrance burst open and Harry didn't slow down but sped through it. We entered the next realm.

After the darkness of the tunnel the brilliant sunshine was painfully blinding. I felt Harry screech to a halt and sit down, I let myself fall off his back and plop to the floor. He morphed back and knelt beside me, "You okay?"

"Fine." I rubbed my eyes. The change from the pitch black to the bright light had really surprised me and my head was spinning like a carousel. I managed to sit in a half up right position, squinting up into his face which was shielding me from the sun, his smile almost as radiant. His nose scrunched up into a cat-like face and he moved away, leaving me blinded.

"You stink!" What a mood killer.

"Huh?"

"You fell in the sewer, you stink!" He was serious about the smell. I checked my hair and smelt the most awful stench of unmentionables.

"I bet you smell worse. You're a guy." That was almost the most stupid and sexist thing I had ever said. Struggling to sit up, I asked, "Where are we?"

"We're Nowhere."

SONG IN THE BLISSFUL LIGHT

Once my eyes had adjusted to the light I looked around and saw millions of flowers. And a sound like bees humming rang in our ears. As I concentrated on it more I could make out words. Small, soft, melodic words. I heard a love song, a melody full of sorrow and basses full of pain. They were the Singers. "At least they haven't started reading my thoughts yet." I whispered to myself, remembering something I had read in the diary about the songs telling all who listened what you were thinking. I stood and stared at the vast circle of flowers surrounding me. All different colours and petal shapes. Breathtaking. I knelt beside one and watched as it bent and sang in the wind. Harry knelt by another one and gently stroked it. I did the same. He muttered something to it but I couldn't hear what he was saying. It sounded like he was chanting, or trying to sing along with the bloom. His voice drifted towards me on the wind and I could hear the words softly but clearly.

"Sweet love, my dear,
Please stay near,
For my heart depends
On You

Keep me in your arms,
So that you will
Never go far
Away."

The sweet melody hypnotized me and the breeze almost lifted me off the ground and into the clouds. I realized that I was watching his every move. As he sung the words the flowers hummed.

"That was beautiful," I murmured, too dazed to say anything more. Harry stared into the flower seeming to look for a response. All he came up with was, "Uh, thanks," but you still have to give him credit for singing in front of critical old me.

"Where d'you learn to sing like that?" I crossed my arms against my chest, getting a little uncomfortable around the extremely hot - I mean Harry.

He seemed to be shifty too, "My dad," he muttered as he got up from kneeling, not looking at me. He didn't seem to want to talk about the subject so I thought it would be a good idea to drop it. But when have I ever followed along with a sensible, good idea?

"Did he teach you or is it in your blood?" I ran up beside him, pushing for an answer.

"Genes." One word answers were becoming a thing with him. Well, I wasn't going to let that happen.

"What was he like, a popular singer or something?" I persisted.

"'Guess so." Great, two words.

"Anybody I would know?"

"Possible, his name was Devin Shifter."

"Oh my gosh, Oh my gosh! You are not telling me your father is the Body Shifter. He is the most amazing dancer/singer in the world." The words were falling out of my mouth before I could close it. Sorry flowers, word puke coming right down at you. He flashed a smile at the ground and kept walking towards whatever he thought was the right direction.

"We've done a lot of walking so far. Is it going to be like this the whole time? Let's sit down and eat. I'm hungry," I plopped down on the dusty grass and flung my backpack in front of me. Harry came and sank next to me. I guessed he had no objection to the nosh. "Let's see, what did I pack?" I scrabbled around in there for a while until I found the t-shirt I had stuffed the food into, "Okay, we have Oreos,"

"Yum."

"We have some homemade bread, credit to Bernie, and we have some peanut butter. Oh, and some water." I pulled it all out as I listed it.

"Is that it?" he knew the answer to that already. He lifted his head to the sun and closed his eyes.

"Yeppers. We have to save the rest for later. For now, dig in, buddy. I'm going to do an experiment." I grabbed a piece of bread and sort of made a crease in it so that there were two halves. Then I picked up a couple of Oreos, opened them up and spread the cream on one of the halves of bread. I popped the cookie parts into my mouth, crunching loudly for effect. I felt like I was on one of those 'learn-how-to-cook-on-tv- shows. I explained everything to Harry as

I went along. "And then you spread some peanut butter on the other side, fold it up and *voila!* You have yourself a PBOC. Peanut butter and Oreo cream sandwich." I took a giant bite out of my new culinary achievement, then gagged it back up again. "Aw, yuck! Not going in the recipe book." I managed to swallow another bite, then realized how hungry I truly was and ate it all. While I was preparing my second PBOC, I looked up at Harry. He was enjoying a peanut butter sandwich with some Oreos for dessert. Wimp. I glared at him while I "cooked", not realizing when I cut my finger on the knife I was using to spread. When I saw the blood it immediately started to sting. I guess peanut butter is not the best cuts and sores medicine. I grimaced and, with one hand, searched my bag for a plaster. I fiddled with the wrapping for a while until Harry took it off me and gently placed it around my bloody finger. It had dripped down into my half made sandwich, but only a little and I managed to wipe all the visible stuff off. The iron in the blood sure didn't help the taste. I flinched with every chomp. Harry was happily enjoying his food and humming to the song he had sung earlier. I listened to the music and soon, I found myself dreaming. And my dream came true.

PSYCHIC DREAMS AND UP A HILL

I was so confused. I knew it couldn't be possible, but there it was, playing out in front of me. Was I psychic, something to do with being a fire demon? I had no idea. It played out exactly how I dreamed it.

There was a big man, a very menacing man, lurking in the shadows of a huge mountain, so tall that you couldn't see the top of it, for it was hidden in the clouds. He was holding a long metal pole and pointing it at me and Harry. He then pointed to the mountain.

"I think we should follow him." I recited the words I had spoken in my vivid dream.

"You're right. That's Manamecio, Zacheri Smoke's henchman. We definitely shouldn't follow him, but we have to go in that direction. The first Arrow is in there." Like he had in my sleep, he motioned to the mountain. I followed my feet as they started running, I didn't know why at this point, but I did know I just had to keep going, I heard Harry pounding along behind. We both stood panting at the start of the climb, waiting for the other person to brave the first step. Harry was the one to do it. I followed him most of the way up but it got really steep and eventually we were side by side pulling each other along.

He stumbled and yelped. I spun around as fast as possible and tried to catch him but he was out of reach. He slid back down the mountain side towards a jutting-out branch.

"Grab on to that tree!" I screamed at him. He was going so fast, there was no way I could catch him now. He swung out and grabbed at the small tree that stuck out at an angle. "Hold on!" I slid down after him but instead of grabbing the branch, I landed with my feet on top of it. Reaching down to pull him up and holding on with my other hand, we managed to get safely into a little gap between rocks I hadn't noticed on the way up. We sat and panted like blood hounds for several minutes until we simultaneously got up to get going once again. As we progressed the air got smoggy and cloudy. On several occasions, I had to stop to have a small coughing fit. After a couple of hours of hiking, we stopped yet again for some water.

"You did bring water, right?" I was hoping he had, because we had already drunk my supply at lunch time.

"Yeah, of course." He lifted out one of those litre bottles and set it down, along with two small cups so that we could drink like civilized people. "If we run out of water, I'm sure there will be sources somewhere along the way."

I didn't respond but just drank cup after cup. Hiking can really dehydrate you. After a few minutes of both of us not talking but just drinking, we ran out.

"Damn it." He whispered to himself.

"Dude its okay; I'm surprised you lugged this great thing the whole way. You couldn't have brought any more than this."

"It's not that," he shyly replied, "I really need…to go."

"Go where?" At that point in my life, I wasn't really 'down with the lingo', if you know what I mean.

"Ya know, squeeze the lemon, number one, do my business."

"I still don't get it."

"I NEED TO GO TO THE TOILET." He said a little too loudly, in fact we could almost hear an echo.

I snickered but I wasn't going to embarrass him any further, "There's a bush over there." I turned away and heard him get up and scrunch around. There was a yelp and a cry and I spun around once more.

"What?! What happened? What is it?!"

"It was a… thorn bush." Pain filled his throat.

I couldn't help but roll around on the floor in laughter. He got back to his business behind another bush. It was really embarrassing for both of us because I could…hear him, if you know what I mean.

"Okay let's keep going," My mind had wandered and I hadn't heard him come up behind me. Without saying another word, we moved on. A few hours passed and I could hear rumbling. I knew the henchman guy would be ahead of us but he must have stopped as well. You would have to have super powers to walk up a really high mountain in one go. Who knew, he could have been right in front of us. Determined, we moved on. Even though it was bright daylight when we entered the smog, it must have been nearly when we reached the top. The moment we finished our terrible journey, I lay splat on my back and could have fallen asleep if I hadn't felt something creeping up my leg...

"Hey! What the heck is that?"

"Relax, it's just Mister Spider wanting to come and play?" he said childishly with an evil grin shinning on his wide awake face. I immediately jumped up and did the 'get it off me, get it off me' dance while Harry peered over the edge of the hole. His face glowed red like he was mirroring fire. And sure enough, he was. The Hungry Lava.

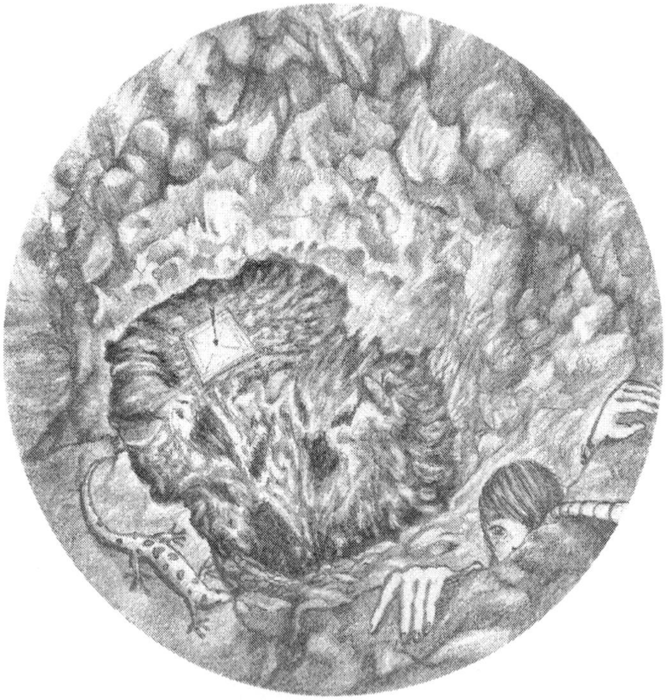

CLIMBING DOWN AND ERUPTING UP

"Read the section on it, Harry." I passed him the book. He took it, not looking away from the heat below.

"At the bottom of the Vicious Volcano, heat springs up creating the smokiest of ash clouds. Far beneath these grey pillows is an angry monster, a hungry monster. The Hungry Lava. As a seeker climbs down the rocky edges of the inner- mountain, the red liquid laps at their heels, burning any normal person. But if a fire demon ever reached this point, they would only feel warm water at their ankles. But they must still be wary of their footing because the man-eating liquid will show no mercy." His reading voice should win a prize. It could lull a screaming baby.

"Good thing I'm fire demon, then." I really am the queen of the obvious.

"I don't think I'm coming down. Here, I brought some rope. I can lower you down and pull you back up. I'm not a body builder so you're going to have to take some of your own weight as well."

I nodded. It would be much easier and safer if only I went down. I came alongside him and looked into the crater. I could see it clearly, the first Arrow. It shone as bright as a star and I let out a little squeal of joy. Just the thought of being one step closer to getting GG back and saving the world made me both anxious and excited. He did the honours of tying the rope around me. And after I had finished giving him a brief lesson on rock climbing commands, he lowered me down.

I had the book in my pocket and wanted to see if there were any other things I needed to know about the volcano.

"Tension!"

"Already?"

As I lay back over the volcano, with Harry straining to hold all my weight – I could hear his struggling grunts - I skimmed through what I had already heard and looked at the section called 'Leopard Lizards'.

"These little black and yellow spotted devils hide in the crevices of rock in the vicious volcano. As an adventurer edges down the spiky climbing wall, they must watch out for these reptiles for if they are bitten on the finger while searching for a hand hold, their hand will go numb for a whole minute, forcing them to hold on with just one hand over the evil death trap below." I looked at another bit that was all underlined.

"A violent place, in the middle of the Nowhere District. The tallest mountain for miles and miles. In the belly of this unpredictable, blasting monster is the very first Arrow. The hiker must make their way up the treacherous volcano to the very top, only to climb down the iniside steep and spiky wall. Once the traveler is safely at the bottom of the volcano, they again must watch their footing because the hungry lava will maneuver around the floating pieces of rock seeking to devour them."

Both passages freaked me out so much, that I got the shivers. These two evil things were lurking far beneath me and I had no choice but to stick my tongue out at them.

"Slack!" I could feel the rope loosen, and I grabbed the wall, holding on hard. The rope was getting longer and longer and I would have to go down at some point. I looked up and saw Harry's face peaking over the side. He must have fixed up some sort of pulley system by attaching it to a tree or something. I gently lowered my foot down, feeling along the wall for the next foot hole. When I found it, I settled in that position for a few minutes. "Maybe this won't be so bad after all," I said to myself. After a few hand holds down, I got the hang of it, until I touched something softer than a piece of rock. "Oh darn." A sharp stinging pain shot through my pointing finger making it instantly numb, and the numbness spread through my whole hand. "TENSION!" I screamed at Harry. He quickly pulled all the rope up and made it tight so that I could almost just sit/stand there holding on with one hand until I could feel the other one again.

As I held on, I watched as the horrible little reptile made its way back into its miniature cave, obviously in a huff because some big human thing had squished him. I kinda felt sorry for him, yet I did take my hand off him as soon as I felt him bite me. And my hand couldn't have been that heavy. I mean, it's just a hand.

As soon as I could feel my fingers I started down again, looking in each hole for any unwanted acquaintances. On more than a few occasions a little sucker popped out and, without getting close enough to get bitten, I shooed them back home. At one point, I got so frustrated with them that I actually kicked one. I think it was dead because when I got to eye level with it, it wasn't moving. I felt guilty the rest of the way down. It took almost a solid two hours to get all the way down to near the bottom. I had to stop several times to catch my breath. As I went further, there were bigger crevices, almost shelves, to rest in. How thoughtful of Mother Nature.

When I was finally a few metres from the lava, I started to get more nervous. I could hear the Hungry Lava jumping at me, and when I hit a slab of rock connected to the wall like a little shore, I was sure it was going to spill over it and swallow me up in one gulp. Untying the cord around my stomach, I looked around the huge cavern. Most of the time when I was climbing down, I had only looked at the wall, definitely not behind me. I stared across the liquid and saw what I should have been expecting but took me completely by surprise and filled me with horror.

Manamecio was staring back at me from the other side of the lava sea. Had he been waiting for me, or did we come down together? Whatever the answer was, we both wanted the Arrow, and both of us were going to do anything to get it. I took a step closer to the edge of the lava and it tried to grab the tips of my shoes. I saw my first opportunity to jump and I took it, onto a small floating flat rock. As soon as I touched it, it began to move away from the slab and around, towards Manamecio. The wind picked up, even though I didn't think it was possible deep inside a volcano, and the flat rock picked up speed. Moving faster and faster towards him, I saw another rock that was moving in the opposite direction. I had only one chance to jump, or I'd either fall in and be eaten or be killed by Smoke's spy. As I leapt, the rock came to a halt right beneath me. Oh, how convenient. I landed on it with a bit of a wobble but quickly regained my balance. My hands gripped the sides, half in the lava. If you haven't realized already, it didn't hurt, since I can do what I want with heat and fire, but the monster pulled at my fingers trying to suck me in. I decided that I couldn't stay there forever and a similar routine like the one on the busy road played out. Except that I was jumping on moving objects above man eating stuff to get to one of the most important objects in the world.

I didn't see Manamecio, but I knew that he was trying to do the same. No doubt, Zacheri would have conducted a thorough job interview to insure an agile and capable henchman. Sooner, rather than later, I made it to the centre platform. I had already seen that there was a rail around it, encircling the Arrow. What I hadn't seen before was that it was spinning. I mean, whirling so fast that if you didn't hold on you would fly off, and even holding on, your feet would lift up from underneath you. Well, I was rotating so fast all I could see was the Arrow right in front of me. All I had to do was reach for it. But if I reached for it, I would have to let go of the rail I was holding onto for dear life.

"Eruption!" A faint whisper came from above. It was

Harry and his small voice must have echoed down here. It was a perfect idea! If I got the fire in the lava to burst up and carry me with it, I would be able to grab the Arrow on the way up. It was going to work out. I knew it.

Conjuring up all my know-how (which was quite small, seeing as I had only been at this for a few days) I let rip a giant part of my mind and lunged forward, letting go of the rails and grabbing the Arrow. As soon as I touched it, two things happened.

A sudden coolness rushed down my spine, making me shiver.

The fire erupted from underneath me.

I was balancing on top of a giant fountain of fire. I had never felt so much adrenaline go through me, ever. It grew and grew until I was level with the edge of the volcano. I jumped off it and landed next to Harry. When I saw him, I lost my concentration and the fire fell. He was lying on the floor. Unconscious.

ANIMALS AND FREAKY DREAMS

"Harry? Harry! What happened?" I had no idea what to do so I slapped him in the face a few times, and he eventually came round but refused to tell me what happened. "Harry, seriously. Don't be a child. Tell me what happened!"

"Fine, fine. Okay. Just shut up, you're giving me a headache." He caressed his head and put on a silly, pathetic, yet really embarrassed face. "Okay, okay. I think I hit my head or something. Give a guy some warning, the next time you burst a volcano in their face. It really hurts." I shuffled over and inspected his head. There was a bump the size of an oversized egg appearing on the left side of his skull.

"Other than a really bad case of dandruff, I think you'll live. Shall we start to venture down?" I stood up as I spoke.

"No. Let's rest here for the night. I'm really tired and most of the day, we've been walking." He grabbed my hand to pull me back down, but instead just held on to it. I stared at him, then at my hand and he let go. After a really awkward silence, I replied:

"Okay fine." And lay down.

My blood and adrenaline were still rushing through

me so I couldn't get to sleep. Instead, I just watched Harry. He fell deeply asleep very quickly and it was kinda funny to see him curl into a little kitten in his dreams, then a rabbit, followed by a number of different animals. I have a phobia of crocodiles, so when he started to look like one I had to get up and do a lap around the volcano edge to get the picture out of my head. When I got back, he was a beagle with an eye patch, adorable. It took all my strength not to kneel down and stroke his head. I ran another lap of the edge and then tried to get to sleep once again. It took a long time, but I eventually I got there and slept deeply.

"Alexis." A gruffy, dream like voice spoke my name in the distance. I woke up with a start.

"Is anyone there?"

"Alexis." It came again.

"Who are you?"

"It is I. Your grandfather." I stood up and did a 360 of my surroundings, but other than Harry there was no sign of any other human life.

"Where are you? What do you want?" I stuttered.

"I am in here," I could feel something cool touch me inside my chest, where my heart was, *"and I want to help you. Don't be afraid of me."* Those five words were definitely not going to stop me from being frightened.

"What do you mean?"

"I am here for you. To ask when you don't know. You may have my diary, but you do not have my mind." I had no answer. There were so many questions that needed

asking but I couldn't pluck one out of the mess of them all. I managed to say that there were too many.

"I understand. But I am always here." His words faded and the cool sensation through my rock solid heart made me shiver once again. With that, the voice was gone and I was awake and alone in the dark.

CLIFF JUMPING

"Alexis, time to get up." Harry moaned as he rolled me over to face the evil sunlight. I immediately rolled back and covered my face with my arms. I had gotten up early every single day for of my life, but always from a nice, safe bed, in a dark room. Most people would think that it would be harder to get up from the nice situation, but if you haven't slept most of the night and the sun is staring you right in the face, you don't really want to get up in an instant.

"Oh, just get stuffed." I moaned and waved my arm at him, with half of my face full of dirt from sleeping face down in it. Harry was offended by the lack of lovely morning person-ness I portrayed.

"You don't have to say stuff like that." He whimpered. He really was quite a baby. I slowly got up from my dent in the ground and moved to grab the bag and change behind the bush. Harry forgot to tell me that was his morning business bush and I yelled when I found out for myself. I quickly moved to a different hedge and changed into a simple brown t-shirt and some khaki shorts. Harry was wearing a dark purple t-shirt with the name of his favorite band written across it, and scruffy jeans.

"Are you sure you're not going to be hot in those?" Even though we were still in deep smog, I could feel the sunlight beating through it.

"Why? Do you think I am?" His cheeky grin appeared; he posed with his arms across his chest and leaned back in fashion model pose. Aw, yuck. I scoffed and began the long walk down. I presumed it would take less time because we could intentionally slide down part of the way. The first hour we just walked at an angle and my thighs began to hurt after a while. Then Harry got a stitch and proposed that we stay in one place for a rest. After that it was mainly sliding between trees. We must have gone down in a different direction to the way we had come up because at one point, I found myself falling, after a slide, off a small cliff. I definitely didn't remember any wall climbing going up. I landed with a thud on my bum, my legs splayed out in front of me.

"OW!" Then I realized that Harry was right behind me. He was going to land in the same place!!! As soon as I thought of this, I log rolled over, and as soon as I log rolled over, Harry landed in the exact dent I had made when I landed.

"OOF!" The breath definitely got knocked out of him. I wondered if any of my butt muscles had split or something because there was certainly a rather painful sting coming from that region. I stood up and tried to straighten, the pain immediately shot up my back like I had stepped on the trigger of a gun pointed at my behind. It seemed that Harry was having the same sort of troubles except he didn't sit back down he just continued to walk, bent over. I followed him in this manner, but then after a while, the pain wore off and we were able to stride normally. Every time we slid after that, we always made sure we knew what was at the end of each slide. There were a couple more cliffs, but both times we managed to grab a tree before we flew off, then easily climbed down the three metre tall rock faces. After two hours of nonstop downward hiking and sliding, we made it to the finish line. We had a small lunch of PBOCs and I reached into my bag to look at the first Ice Arrow. It shone in the midday sun and shimmered like a star. It was extremely cool to the touch and was a refreshing contrast with the heat in my blood that always seemed to be with me these days. It was silver and white and looked just like an arrow, of course. It took my breath away and after a minute or two gently put it back in the bag.

"Where to next?" I jumped when Harry broke the silence. I took out the book.

"Our next riddle is, "Follow the voices of many, to the land of shimmer. Wait for the next moon to rise and fall, then enter the cool at a dive." My face contorted and I looked at Harry quizzically.

"Well, 'the voices of many' must be the flowers. Maybe if we get to higher ground then we'll be able to see a pattern or something." It seemed like a good guess so we climbed back up to a clear patch on the mountain. It wasn't too high up; just right. It was under where the smog started and at the right height to see the sea of flowers. And sure enough, a beautiful group of orange blooms rose higher than the other flowers and were in a consistent line stretching all around the mountain and through a small valley beyond to the horizon. When we climbed down and got nearer, we also found that they were definitely singing the loudest. If you can imagine heavy metal, but strangely mournful, than you're spot on. Most of the way, we had to cover our ears with the palms of our hands, and even then it didn't stop the ghastly sound. I was sure that by the end of the walk I would be deaf, or at least half deaf. Then, I had an idea.

"HARRY!" We had to scream over the music.

"WHAT!?"

"GRIFFIN! TURN INTO A GRIFFIN, THERE WILL BE ROOM ON YOUR BACK FOR ME TO SIT AND YOU'LL BE ABLE TO FLY ABOVE THE NOISE!" I was sure my wording was all muddled up, but he seemed to understand.

"NO CAN DO! I CAN'T DO MYTHICAL CREATURES!"

"Ugh!" I screamed it loud enough so that Harry thought I was blaming him. A question then struck me, why didn't he just turn into a monkey climbing up and down the mountain? It would have been so much easier. I did my best evil eyes at him. He didn't say anything for a long while, and even if he had, I wouldn't have heard him. At long last, we saw a glimmer of hope. No, really, an actual glimmer. Something was shining over a little hill not too far away from us and we ran all the way there. As we stood on the hill and watched the sun reflect over the sea, we were silent and at peace. I hadn't seen a beach since I was five years old, with my parents, and a rush of home sickness, sorrow and happy memories came over me.

I didn't know what Harry was feeling but a spectrum of mixed emotions was on his face too.

"What are you thinking about?" I tried out my theory of being forward, it usually worked.

"Nothing." This time though, it didn't.

As the riddle said, we waited for the moon to rise and fall into the next. Waiting meant sleeping most of the time, or singing with the flowers.

As the sun rose in the morning, the flowers were quiet and the air was completely still. I wondered if some sort of hurricane was coming because I had read that before a tsunami comes, all the water drains away. Maybe it's the same for air movement.

"Maybe we should dive into the water." It sounded stupid but that was what the riddle called for. Harry stood and stripped off his t-shirt. I wasn't expecting to see his six pack and so I was kinda shocked and amused at the same time. Before I could say anything profound though, he ran off to a rock that jutted out towards a darker colored area and dived in. He didn't come back up. Struggling to regain my breath, I ran to the rock diving board and went in after him.

THE VAST

Water engulfed me like I was a caterpillar that couldn't get out of her cocoon. I struggled to swim to the top but it pulled me in, deeper and deeper until my ears popped and burned. I couldn't see anything and a giant water hand was crushing me. But as soon as I felt the agonizing feeling of right-before-you're-about-to-go-unconscious, the water disappeared from around me and I was free. Alive and breathing. Flying above the water surface and on to a cool beach. Next to Harry, who I saw when I rubbed my eyes and looked to my right.

Out of breath, I managed to mouth a "Hey" in his direction. He mouthed one back to me. But how was it possible. I had gone so deep and had come out the other end. Another thing I noticed was that it was already a dark night and the full moon was hanging over us like a giant white chocolate button. Everything was the exact opposite to what we had come from. When I looked behind us, all I could see were dead trees and flowers hanging in dismay. It was a sorrowful sight. And then I stared forward and saw the biggest ship that I bet anyone has ever seen. It stretched so far, I couldn't see the end of it and it was so tall that the top of it was underneath a cloud, just like the Vicious Volcano.

"Look over there." Harry coughed and pointed to a small rowing boat not too far from the shore. I pulled out the book which surprisingly and unexplainably hadn't got wet, and read:

"The Slanting Ship: At exactly 12:00 midnight the ship will turn on its end, standing vertically for one hour, making everything fall to the bottom of the sea. Afterwards, everything returns to normal. It is a giant ship filled with puzzles and mazes, and of course, the Minty Mourners. It is bigger than the Titanic." We grimaced at the same time. I stared at the little boat and contemplated skipping the second Arrow. This was way different to the volcano. Just the thought of getting lost or being separated in this hunk of metal nearly reduced me to madness. The very idea of being inside the monster of a ship freaked me out. The water made me feel dizzy, so I was sure I'd have countless sea sick related experiences off the side of the boat. I felt all queasy inside and was about to have one of those experiences that moment, when Harry interrupted and stopped my stomach from hurling.

"Read everything about the ship. We need to be prepared." He ordered. On any other day I would have bit back at being bossed, but he was right so I didn't bother.

I skimmed through it before I read it out loud.

"Minty Mourners: on the Slanting Ship the ghosts of voyagers rest, waiting for a body to fill. When one comes along, they instantly smell it and rush to investigate. They use tricks and persuasion to make the new voyager feel utter sympathy and let the mourners take over their body. Once they have a body, they will either devour it out of hunger, or escape the cruise and live like a human. If they choose neither of these, and stay as a human on board, the other ghosts will try to take the body, and so it will be passed around, being persuaded off each soul. The mourners are immortal, but their main weakness is a horror of very loud sounds.

The Ticker: A time lord that could travel in time within a day using a special pendulum. It was built to erase mistakes when world leaders had arguments or agreed on a bad idea. But Zacheri Smoke stole it and turned it in to an ultimate killing machine and placed it on the Slanting Ship to guard an Arrow. If someone takes the pendulum which hangs around its neck, then the Ticker will be motionless for two minutes, giving the attacker time to either run or get the Arrow and hide. It has a human structure, but has dates, clocks and times imprinted all over its body and black, old fashioned clothes. Its eyes are two clocks. It speaks in the voice of whoever it heard last…"

Okay, that was freaky. I had not been expecting that much freaky in a paragraph of writing. It sounded worse out loud than it would have in my head. I couldn't control my voice to emphasize the words in the right/wrong places. Right, being how it was supposed to be read, and wrong because I definitely didn't want to hear it that way. Neither of us did. I could tell from Harry's terrified face. I hoped he wouldn't be too vulnerable for the Mintys to take advantage of. He almost looked sorry for them. That was exactly what they wanted. Well, I certainly wasn't going to feel sorry for body stealers anytime soon.

"Do you reckon we should go?" I hoped he would say no, but as always, he said the complete opposite. "Aw, come on Harry! Let's just skip this one." I whined.

"Oh, and just pick up a normal arrow filled with a magic person's heart on the way to the third? Grow up, Alexis."

"What's with the harsh tone? Don't you care that you could die?"

"Of course I do! But I'd do it to save the world. Don't you care about anybody but yourself?" He yelled at me. I didn't find the words to reply. I had been being selfish. Only caring that it was dangerous for me, when the world was already in danger. But how could I say this to Harry. He would probably have smirked and would use it as an example to say that he was always right. No way was I going to let that happen. My pride was the one part of me that hadn't been intruded on in my life so far, and it was not going to be stepped on by Harry. I dragged myself to the shore line and made shapes in the sand. I planned to procrastinate as much as possible so that I could think of some way of getting the Arrow without going through the Ticker. It was what scared me the most, not that I get scared easily.

I drew a picture of one of the flowers in the Nowhere District. Then the volcano in the background, then a whole field of them. Each had a characteristic; anger, pain, happiness, anxiousness, sadness and random. I didn't notice Harry come and sit by me. He added some more flowers with other emotions and a sun. It was a pretty good picture, actually. Harry drew a line next to it and started a picture of where we were. I didn't know what to call the place. It was obviously the opposite to the Nowhere District, but we couldn't really call it the Somewhere District. It was sad and lonely, all bark and no flower or leaf. I asked Harry about this and he paused from his sand finger drawing.

"Um, I don't know, The Vast. Yeah, the Vast. I think it kind of fits it." He gestured to everywhere around us. I had to agree with him; all we could really see was a vast land of dead trees and a vast ocean. "Look, I know you don't want to, but we have to. It's one of those things where we don't have a choice. So, come on." He said in a quiet tone. I usually don't fall for persuasive speakers, but he was right. I had to stop him from being right all the time. It wasn't… right. I had to be right sometime, ya know.

"It's going to be really dangerous, it isn't about physical ability this time. It's about keeping our strength, not giving in." I was right about that.

"I think I'm going to swim there. Sneak in. You can be the distraction. I'm not a human, they won't smell me." He wasn't quite on target this time.

"No. Way." Those two words were all I was going to say, "I think we should go in full on, battle of wits, kind of like what you said." I knew it was a good idea, but I actually wanted him to have a better idea.

"You do realize that you're contradicting yourself. You're-"

"How am I contradicting myself?!"

"Well, you just made it clear that you're terrified, but

now you're saying that you want to hit it head on!" The truth was, I was really terrified, I just didn't want to be the distraction, possibly dying alone and he would sneak in. For the first time in a while, I took out my key that I usually hid under my shirt and squeezed it tightly. I held it up into the moonlight and inspected it. It was rusty as always, but had a slight shine on the long part. It looked almost gold with the color the rust was giving off. Harry once again sat by me and held it in his hand. In a whisper he said, "Where did you find this?" The wonder in his eyes scared me. Did he know something about it that I didn't?

"It is the only thing I have that my parents gave me. I have worn it since I was a baby and it was on my neck the morning that they disappeared. Why, what do you know?" He moved away from me as I said the last part. He dropped the key back to my chest and stood up.

"Nothing." He started wading out to the boat and I could do nothing but follow. Follow him towards what I thought was going to be my last night.

EVIL SEAWEED

My arms were getting tired. Rowing was much harder than I thought it would be and the distance from the beach to the ship was further than it originally seemed. As we rowed under the moon I thought about our situation. We were two kids, told, by a possibly crazy lady, to go save the world. We were about to enter a really dangerous place full of ghosts and a time lord. I was feeling just peachy. Harry recognized this but didn't say a word, just gave me a sad companion glance. A small current hit the boat and it rocked gently. I gave Harry a quizzical look but just assumed it was a wave. It hit again, a little bit harder. Harry and I looked over each side of the boat simultaneously. We both saw nothing. So, again I assumed that it was just a wave. We were almost knocked out the third time and I immediately looked over to catch a glimpse of whatever it was. I presumed that there would be fish in the sea, like most people would, although I didn't think a salmon would be able to almost flip a medium sized fishing boat. I kept watching till I saw a glimmer of something. It could have been the sparkling water, but I did see something.

"Oh dear." With those two words, Harry gripped

onto his ears like he wanted to rip them out. I did the same. Then I heard it, the screeching. It sounded like something was piercing a sharp needle through a squealing pig, amplifying it through speakers and playing it over and over like a siren. It. Was. Deafening. I felt both my ear drums pop at the same time and then my ears started to ring. The pain was overwhelming. I wanted to scream but as I opened my mouth, Harry's hand gripped it shut. His face contorted into a mass of pain and many different animals popped around it. He would have gone mad if it hadn't stopped soon after.

"What is that?!" It sounded like I was talking really softly, but I knew that I was almost screaming. My eardrums came back after about twenty minutes.

"In the Nowhere District, they have the Singers. Here, they have the Deafeners. They usually go on for longer, I don't know why they stopped." He looked around nervously.

"Number 1; where are they? Number 2; what are they? aAnd number 3; why are they doing this?"

"They're under the water, seaweed monsters and they want to eat us." He said matter-of-factly.

The boat rocked yet again and I gripped the sides.

"Best not to have your fingers near the edge, Alexis." I pulled them in quickly. The dingy softly shifted like a swing and creaked like in an old scary movie. My mind said *keep rowing* but my hands wanted to hide in my pockets. Harry was brave enough to hold on to all four oars like they were his teddy bears, but he didn't row.

"Maybe we should keep going." I said it but I didn't move a muscle. Neither did he. A jolt hit us and I was sure we were going to tip. And the noise started again, as well as a strong current swashing our boat from side to side like it was tossing pasta. I thought about rowing with my elbows, since I would be busy with my hands over my ears, but still I was paralyzed by the terror. Suddenly, the water started moving in a circle around us. We fell.

Down in to the deep, dark, piercing water, surrounded by a slimy monster that thought our flesh was a deluxe breakfast buffet. This was the second time I had been in the water that day. The Deafeners were squeezing and pulling us in all different directions. My shorts and shirt were torn and I could feel the sting of wounds in salt water. The blood floated past my face, slightly warming the ever freezing water. I felt alone, the fall seemed endless. Too endless. The water was engulfing me. I guessed Harry was flying above when the boat fell from beneath us. I closed my eyes and hit the bottom.

I reckoned it was the sand I'd hit, then the water would crush me like an elephant stamping on an ant. Moving my arms over my head, I braced for the rush of pressure, not that it would help. Death was quick and painless, heck, it only felt like somebody pouring a bucket of water over my head. Oh wait, that's actually what happened. I rolled over to face up and look around at what I thought was heaven. What I saw was a giant ballroom lit up with a beautiful chandelier of crystals and candles. It wasn't what I expected, but it would have to do for the rest of eternity. The next thing I saw was quite surprising.

"Harry? You're dead too?" I sounded like I was speaking in a dream. But I could have just had a lot of water blocking my ears.

"You are not dead, idiot."

"Don't need to be so harsh, Mister Water Bucket." I noticed he was holding the wet weapon.

"When you hit the bottom, you fainted. I grabbed you and flew up. We're on the ship. This was the first empty room I could find. Girl, you are not the lightest person, you know." He sounded like he was talking about an assault course he had to do while carrying me on his back. He was definitely understating what he had done for me. I wanted to jump up and give him a big smacker on the lips. But I resisted the urge because a) ewww!! b) superewww and c) my legs hurt from falling so far. I checked myself over for damage. I had a really big slash at the top of my left arm and one below my right knee. Both of them stung like mad. I noticed Harry kneel down beside me. I also noticed that he wasn't wearing his shirt. The next thing I knew, he was tearing it up and tying it around my cuts. My body had no strength to fight him off, all I did was give a small whimper and lie back down. The world seemed to be spinning upside down and all over.

"The Deafeners were attacking you as you went." He patched me up and pulled me to my feet which made everything turn even faster. I made sure Harry could hear me groan. "You're welcome." He breathed.

It then hit me. We were on the Slanting Ship. And it was almost midnight. The time for the ship to go vertical and for us to fall to the bottom of the sea.

Again. "Thank you for saving me from one death trap to another, Harry."

LUCA

There was a clock above the door of the ballroom. It read 10:45. We had an hour and fifteen minutes to get through the Minty Mourners, find our way across the ship without getting lost, get past the Ticker, find the Arrow and get the heck out of there. Okay, this was going to be a blast. Harry crept towards the door and peeked out.

"All clear," He whispered. I crept equally quietly and peeked out below him. Nothing there.

"Okay, let's move." It was like an old, black and white, predictable spy movie. As soon as we turned the corner, I ran into (or rather, ran through) none other than, a Minty Mourner.

"Hello there." A sad, raspy and dreamy voice didn't come from his lips.

"Uh, hi and bye." We ran past, in my case through again, and kept running till we got to another corner.

"Hello, once again." He was there again.

"He must have come around a different way." I whispered through my teeth to Harry in front of me.

"My name is Luca. What's yours?" He actually

sounded friendly. I figured we may be able to trust him. Even if he was following us and his kind was known for stealing bodies. His eyes were a beautiful color, I couldn't put my finger on what it was and his curly hair was a light blonde. I noticed he was holding a football.

"It's Alexis." I came forward. As I got closer I noticed that he looked about our age. He didn't seem like somebody who would steal a body.

"That is a nice name, want to play some footy?"

"Sorry, we're kind of on a tight schedule." Harry was the one to answer this time. He started to move away but Luca floated in front of him.

"Are you looking for the Timer?"

"You mean the Ticker?"

"Yes, I know a fast route. Come." Harry held me back.

"We cannot trust him. Don't fall for it." It was obvious that he was dubious of Luca, but I didn't say anything.

"I think we can trust him." And I walked on behind him, leaving Harry in my dust. In my mind, I really hoped that he was following because I was only 75% sure of Luca, but I resisted looking back.

"Thank you for believing me." We had been marching for a while, and none of us had spoken. Luca broke the silence, fortunately. "All the people that have ever come here, I have helped. I like it here and I don't want to take anybody else's life away. That is just cruel." A smile crept across my face. Harry probably rolled his eyes at it, but I thought Luca's statement was sweet. A question popped into my mind. I opened the book to the Minty Mourners page and looked for his name. And sure enough, there it was at the bottom of the page. It said "Look for Luca, he'll help."

I lifted it above my head so that Harry would be able to see and gave the floor a smug grin. An annoyed sigh came from behind. We went down staircases and through long hallways. A few times, I heard parties in rooms as we passed. I was surprised that they couldn't smell our human... smell. Luca seemed to have read my mind.

"I am covering your body stench. Do not worry. They are busy partying." He seemed annoyed with the others. I wondered why.

"There are hardly any other cruisers my age. They all treat me like I'm a child." I was really wondering if he could read my mind.

"I can." That answered that question.

"Grandpa never mentioned that Minty Mourners could read minds." I stated.

"That's because I was like this before I lost my body. He was writing about all the cruisers in general." I was surprised. Was he something...else? I mean, Grandpa gave the impression that the Minty Mourners were all bad. And Luca kept calling them cruisers.

"I was a Singer." It sounded like he was just stating what ice cream flavor he had last night. I was really confused.

"Singers can read minds. They don't always tell you. One day, a long time ago, a gypsy came to Nowhere. She wanted my handsome colors and so she took them away from me. When you're a dull flower in the District, they throw you out here on this boat. There are only a few others though." I felt so sorry for him. Failing, I tried to put my hand on his shoulder. It just slipped through and looked like I'd tried to hit him. I thought in my mind of what I tried to do and he gave me an understanding smile. Harry grabbed my arm and spun me around.

"Don't fall for it. He's trying to make you feel sorry for him."

"Harry, if he wanted a body, he would want to be a Singer again. How could I give him that, even if I did fall for his persuasion?" He dropped his hand and sighed once more. We walked on.

ANUSHA

Luca jolted to a stop at a point between me being exhausted and being infuriated that we hadn't arrived at the Ticker's door yet.

"Be very quiet." Luca whispered. While we walked, I had thought about how Luca's mouth didn't move when he talked. I figured this was because he was speaking inside our heads. It was silly to whisper when our minds could hear him. I thought back, *okay. Why?* No response came from football boy.

Not long after we stopped, I heard a soft whooshing sound coming from behind a door. It sounded like a fan that had slowed down. It really freaked me out. Luca turned to Harry, but I couldn't hear anything. I looked from Harry to Luca, they seemed to be having an expression war. I immediately felt left out. Luca was talking to Harry without me. Not cool.

"Dudes, what is it?" I said in a hushed tone, but not quietly enough. As soon as Luca put a finger to his lips the door flew open and a dark floating thing lurked out. Her face was solemn and sad, but a hint of fiery hatred burned in her eyes.

"Luca, you didn't tell me we had guests." She spoke from her mouth, rather than through her mind. Luca looked like a little boy who had just been caught reading under the covers with a flash light. She glared at me, as if I were the devil's spawn, but with a forced, plastic smile. I thought they wanted to trick us into giving ourselves up to them, not scare us away. Maybe she was trying the faking-to-be-so-angry-but-dying-inside approach. Like Harry said, neither of us was going to let either fall for any ghost's tricks.

All I could think to say was, *we come in peace,* but I decided that wasn't really appropriate.

"They have come for the Arrow." Luca muttered in her ear. It was the first time we had seen him talk out loud through his mouth. Even though that's how most beings make noise, we were surprised. When you hear something in your head, you don't really hear the accent, but Luca had a very thick one out loud. She nodded at what he had said, but never took her eyes off me. I felt the piercing pupils burning through my skin. It actually hurt to hold her stare. It was almost like she was challenging me not to look away. I finally couldn't handle it anymore and dropped my eyes to the floor. I could feel her evil smile beam down at me. That was another thing. She had floated about thirty centimetres above the ground so throughout the stare down, I had to look up at her.

"Come with me." She said in a sinister slicing tone. She flicked her wavy hair as she spun around and air-strode down the hallway. This time I was hesitant, yet she didn't seem to have any desire for me either, so I hurried along behind Luca. I hadn't checked to see what Harry was thinking about all this, but I guessed it was not happy thoughts.

We walked for yet another long distance and I was really getting paranoid about the time. Everything seemed to be going so slow since we got on the boat, as if all the adrenaline had been pumped *out* of everything. Luca must've been listening in on my head and decided to walk along beside me instead of in front. It was kind of awkward because the hallway wasn't wide enough for both of us to have personal space side by side, so half of his 'body' was in the wall. This made me feel even weirder.

"Do you want to know the time?" He held out his pocket watch to me. It read only eleven o'clock! How was that possible; it felt like we had been walking for over an hour already. "For a human, the ship takes away a lot of your energy so that you will be more vulnerable to the Minty Mourners." I hadn't realized before that the ship and the Mintys were joined forces. I mean, I knew they were both dangerous but much worse together.

"I see." I said out loud, forgetting the silent code. Luca had told me her name was Anusha. Suddenly, without any warning, the menacing silent figure lurched in front of me and tried to grab me with her ghostly hands only to fall through me. It was like her eyes were guns and she was shooting out rays of heat. I wondered if I could do that with fire. I didn't really have time to experiment since she was trying to burn a hole through my head. A hand grabbed me and we ran.

"She'll kill you if a Minty finds out she's helping you. Run to the side of the boat and jump. I'll find you later." Luca echoed in my head and sure enough at the end of the hall way was a door leading out to a view of the moon. Harry didn't slow down when we got to the door. He just slammed right through it, obviously hurting his head. And without looking back, we flung ourselves off the side.

MINTIES WANT OUR BODIES

The taste of chlorine when I hit the surface of the pool made my head grow dizzy. I was expecting salt water. I had closed my eyes for the fall, but I opened at the last minute to see the water. When we flew off I thought we'd land in the sea, but instead we landed in a private swimming pool. Harry scrambled about and finally clambered out of the water. Only then did he realize that there weren't any Deafeners trying to eat him in the pool. He gave out a huge sigh of relief and looked around for me. I was still floating in the water, staring up at him. I didn't feel like moving ever again. I hoped Harry would read my mind that time and lift me out of the water and over his shoulder. But instead, being the jerk he was, he motioned for me to get out and stalked off down a short flight of stairs. Feeling drugged, I forced myself to swim to the bars and climb out.

"Harry, wait up." I half whispered, half yelled. Sluggishly slumping down the stairs, I saw a figure move past me. Then another. And another. "Harry?... Harry, I think we're surrounded." No answer. "Harry?"

"Sweety." An old woman's voice that I recognized

immediately broke the terrifying silence of being alone. "They took mine, will you give me yours?" How could I resist GG? I turned to look at her, but instead saw a terrifying thing. An old hag stood before me. Her teeth askew, sticking out like fangs. Her hair was like a mane spreading out in so many different directions and covering her eyes, which still shone through, blue as sapphires and bright like torches. The hands that were outstretched had skin folding over each, much like her sinking expression. And her clothes were all black. "Spare a body for an old lass." She hissed through her teeth, giving up GG's voice and using her own raspy voice. Employing some colorful cursing, I departed from the room through a square door. I slammed against the wall to hide. There was a window in the door and I risked a peep through it. There was nothing there and I let out a huge sigh. I almost screamed when something touched my arm and a hand gripped my mouth.

"Shush! It's me." Harry had a crazed look in his eyes like he'd just been through absolute disaster, around the world and back. His now ginger hair was a mess and he definitely didn't care. I shushed and leaned back against the wall.

"Don't. Do. That. Ever again. Got it?" I was in crazy mode too, and I wasn't letting him get away with it.

He ignored me, "There are more. Lots more. Luca told me that he'll meet us under the pool."

"We went down a flight of stairs, so there must be some rooms under it."

"But they're out there." His voice cracked in the

middle of his sentence.

"I think we just have to go out there and ignore them." I said this because Grandpa said they were dangerous with their tricks, not physically. But my mind flipped back to Anusha.

His hand reached out towards the door handle, pulled back, then went for it again. His arm was left hanging as he latched on to the handle, not turning or retracting. Just staying limp with terror. I had had enough and pushed his hand down flat so that the door flung open right through the ghost who was waiting behind it. Whoops. That did not make her happy.

"Jenna, not happy." Her blue eyes flipped to purple and her voice changed to a deep caveman like one. Harry gave me the eyes that told me to run around the pool looking for a door and that he would try to keep her occupied. We were getting used to speaking with our expressions. Heck we might have been brilliant actors, if we hadn't agreed to go along with this crazy adventure.

I did what I was told and zoomed like wild fire, running past horrible looking ghosts with pleading and sadness in their furiously bright eyes. I went through so many cold floaters; so many that I couldn't count. Doing a full lap of the pool, I didn't see any doors but that was because most of the time I was shielding my eyes going through dead souls wanting to take away my body. Once again, racing around the base of the private pool, I saw a small door, shorter than me.

"HARRY, I FOUND ONE!" I screamed at the top

of my lungs; this would definitely attract more Mourners but soon we'd be masked by Luca so I didn't mind. Harry came running at full speed with his arms covering his face, much like I did, scared of the freezing feeling of going through an angry soul. He banged into me, didn't even say sorry, and tried to kick open the door. He failed miserably and hurt his foot. I calmly slid between him and the door and turned the handle, gracefully stepping in. One of us had to be collected, even though I was screaming at him in my head to get inside and that it wouldn't matter if we were in or not because they could just skip in past the walls.

It was a small closet with a hanging light switch. I gave out a tiny yelp of joy when I heard a familiar voice in my head. Looking beside me, I saw Luca.

"Are you two okay?" He asked, clearly concerned. He had grey slashes across his cheeks, like somebody with really sharp nails had scraped him across the face. Anusha had really long nails. I realized he had stayed back and taken the blame for my idiocy. I sent out a million thank you's in his direction. He pushed them all aside with a humble mutter. The cupboard was so small that I could feel Harry shivering with fear beside me. It made me shiver too.

"They're moving away. They think you two disappeared because they can't smell you anymore. They are not the brightest bunch" Luca sent to me. I chuckled silently and I think Harry loosened up a bit. He went on, "There is another door beneath us, and it falls into the room in front of the Ticker's. I'm afraid I cannot help you after that." That started Harry up once again. Why couldn't Luca help us inside?

"Because I am afraid." He said this out loud. And I knew he had done enough for us, I couldn't ask him to do this. He pulled what I thought was the light switch and Harry and I fell on to a couch directly underneath. How convenient. Then a noise came from behind a door in front of us. A clock noise. *Tick tock, tick tock.*

TICKER, SAILOR, SOLDIER, DIE

Neither of us moved, frozen still on the bright red couch we had landed on. We could hear the menacing ticking getting louder and louder, coming towards the door. Both hearts were pounding like drums building up to a big finale. The final finale. We watched as the knob turned slowly, creaking ever so quietly, although it sounded like thunder to us in the silent room. It may seem cliché to you, but my life really did flash before me. I saw the last night I ever saw Mum and Dad, the first day I ever completed the assault course without falling over or hurting myself. Those things seemed meaningless irrelevancies to the moment coming towards me. My death. Why had I been alive if I was going die so early and horribly? I didn't know, and I thought I would never know. The door flew open but I couldn't see anything. A slight gasp escaped my lips when I realized I had been holding my breath. Something behind the wall stood and footsteps came. I hated myself for that tiny sigh and regretted it for the rest of my life. I found out later that the Ticker had fallen asleep. When he heard a thud, he opened the door, but didn't see anything. As he drifted back into a deep sleep, the gasp awakened him from his almost-slumber and he was angry.

Angrier than the sun when the moon steals it's thunder. Eight ticks later, he appeared at the entrance. Using up the last of my strength, I stood and we faced each other across the room. His body was just as it was written; all black clothes, his eyes; clocks, and time all over. Pure hatred was written on his tattooed face. I noticed Harry grabbed my hand and was trembling so hard that his skin looked like it was jumping off of his body. Or maybe it was me, I couldn't tell. Harry face reflected the fear on my face and we stared at each other as the Ticker approached us. A glimmer of something familiar was in his eyes. He looked at me like my parents used too and how GG had at some moments. Could it have been –

"Restricted area. Leave or be terminated." He interrupted my thinking. His voice was metallic, he must not have heard anybody in a long time otherwise he would have spoken like them.

"No." I managed to say it really high-pitched and almost like a question. Harry was surprised at my courage for saying even one word. The Ticker repeated what he had said and raised his arm and waved towards another door behind us, as if he was a military machine, except still human-like. Weirdly enough, we stood our ground, partly because we were too scared to move, and partly because the couch was the width of the room. Harry took a brave step forward. I don't know why because it just made him tremble even harder, but I would also be thankful for that step he took. Because if he hadn't taken that step, he might not have accidently kicked the Ticker's shin giving me the chance to run past. The reason why I knew it wasn't on purpose was because I actually heard Harry apologizing for smashing him while coming forward. I ran into the room, panting even though I only went a few strides. And there it was, the second Arrow. The brightness of the bronze danced on the walls in the dimly lit room. It was balanced on its tip at an altar like table with two bright burning red candles. Again, how convenient. Hoping it wasn't a trick, edging towards the altar and making sure the Ticker wasn't at the door, I edged towards the little shrine. My hands were shaking as I reached for the beautiful bronze Arrow. But it slipped through my fingers.

My back smashed into the wall, definitely bruising my spinal cord or something. We had gone sideways in a flash and I was lucky the altar hadn't dropped on top of me. It was nailed to the floor. But the Arrow wasn't.

In the room behind me, I heard the couch, Harry and the Ticker fly backwards. I crawled to the door, which was now a window looking downwards. The Ticker was already standing up (he had probably known exactly when everything was going to move sideways, since he was a human clock) staring over Harry who was still lying on the floor rubbing his head. Neither of them looked pleased. I watched, with terror, the scene that played out.

The Ticker opened the curtains and with crisp hostility he barked, "Prepare for combat."

Harry stood up, not a happy bunny, and got into the most threatening position he could. He took the first move. A high kick to the face that resulted in him just hurting his foot on the rock solid head of the evil time lord. I jumped in, "FIND HIS WEAKNESSES, YOU ALREADY KNOW THE SHINS!" I hoped the Ticker would ignore me and continue to beat up Harry. He went for them, but not in time because Mr. Bad Guy had swung a right hook at him. I saw a flash of red on Harry's face as he dropped to the floor. The silence was intense. Anguish overflowed my heart as I watched Harry crumple and cover his face. It seemed like he was unconscious. There was nothing I could do. It was a ten metre long room so a ten metre drop from where I was.

But as I watched, something miraculous happened. Harry was morphing, and this time, something bigger than himself. Something majestic and golden. He was a lion. He slowly stood up on the wall now turned floor and glared at the Ticker. It did not show any emotion, but it took a few steps back indicating it wasn't too sure about having a giant cat staring him down. I felt like shouting "GO HARRY!" At the top of my lungs but that could have ruined the whole action scene being played out.

Harry, the Lion, lunged forward, teeth bared, towards the legs of the surprised Ticker. A roar escaped its voice box, I guessed it only knew two emotions; anger and pain. A lump of its human skin was peeled off by Harry's teeth and you could see the copper wiring inside, all rusted from not being used or attacked in so long. He clutched his pendulum, but it just gave off sparks. Had Harry damaged his time travelling powers? Well, that made everything much easier. He still had to fight the infuriated monster of a clock, though. All his times were ticking double time like they were his heartbeat, pounding under the rush of adrenaline.

It was time to think fast, like the Ticker's pulse, about what else would be his weaknesses. I tried to flashback to when I did a whole unit on medical training in the field. What other bones were a similar structure to the shin? It was a useless question when I was learning it, but really helpful at that moment. I scanned my mind but I couldn't remember anything. I decided to go with the opposite of the leg, "TRY THE ARM!" Harry was already way ahead of me. He pounced to the side and swiped at the mechanical killer. It crumpled under the weight of his paw, electricity giving it tiny spasms. It was horrible, lying on the floor still as death.

Harry switched to a bird and flew up. He perched beside me and shifted back. "You okay?" I was concerned, his nose was still bleeding and he limped.

"I'm fine. Did you get the Arrow?"

I felt. Really. Stupid. How could I have forgotten about the only reason we were there? Running around the wall searching in every bit of the room, I couldn't find it.

"Alexis, you're an idiot." Harry stated not making me feel any better. I told him this but also noticed he was staring down through the door. I crawled over to look too and I regretted it.

The Ticker was holding the Arrow in his hand and grinning like an evil bob cat. "Come and get it." He laughed in a sing-song voice.

I hated being mocked and I wasn't going to stand for it. Throwing my legs over the side, kicking off the side of the wall and landing on the cushiony couch, I faced him.

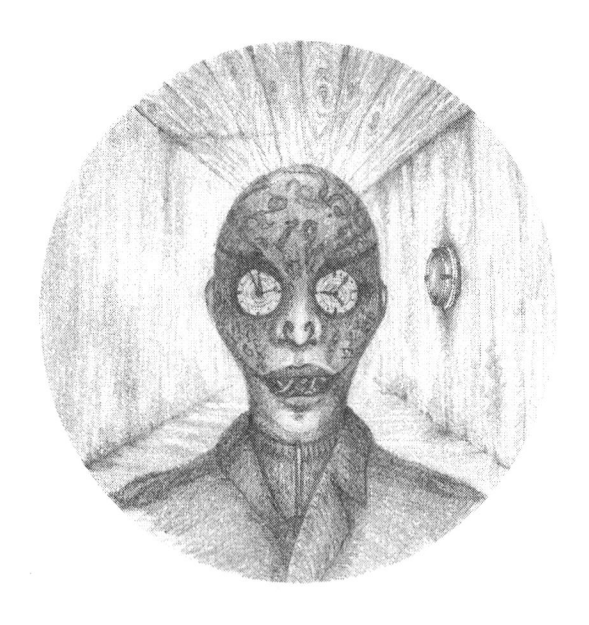

FIRE AND TIME

It was like an old cowboy movie. Facing each other at about ten paces. A brain wave flashed through me; his pendulum didn't work but there was fire in the next room. My fingers twitched as I tried to summon the fire to me. Harry read my mind and threw down the candles. They somehow kept alight. I grabbed them as they fell and felt the brilliant burn of the flickers. I threw away the sticks and held the red lights in my palms. He twitched with electricity once again, and then the fight began.

At first, I was feeling slightly cocky, thinking that he had no powers since his pendulum wasn't working, and that I would succeed easily by burning him to a crisp. Little did I know that he not only could he move steps forwards or backwards in time, but he could just make it go faster for him, meaning that he could swing faster, dodge faster and run faster. My face; annoyed and flustered with fury. His face; metallic and full of anger. I knew this was going to be a hard fight, so I mustered up the most fearsome face I could and prepared for the epic battle. Well, not so epic for the loser, whoever it was going to be. I hoped not me.

It was time to start and I slowly pulled up all the fire atoms I could find in the tiny flickers and enlarged them, making a bright furnace, heavy in my arms. The Ticker put his arms in front of his clock eyes to guard them from the intense heat and light. Good, he wasn't able to see me. I waved my arms in a circle, building up momentum, and then threw the fire with all my strength. I thought that it would just wound him, but it blew all of his fake skin right off his robot metal body. The sight was horrible, all glitches and clocks gadgets; my mind was spinning watching all the whirring parts.

I pulled my eyes away and continued in my attempt to destroy the horrible creature. My first attack was great, blowing his flesh off and all, but my second …not so good. I decided to go for a more human approach, instead of using powers, and I went for a high kick to the stomach. Like I said before, he was faster and grabbed my foot and spun my whole body around and around, like a crocodile does, under the water, in order to drown its prey. In my case, he was trying to make my head fall off from being so dizzy. Thankfully, he let go, throwing me onto the wall/floor. I slumped down and pretended (it's what I do best) to be unconscious. If he had spun me any more times, I would have been. The notorious big clock marched over like a robot. I guess since he lost his human appearance, he wasn't going to bother acting like a person. He bent down and I heard the '*Whirrrr, click!*' that came from his machinery in his backside. I panicked as he pulled his arm back for one last swing at my face, which I was sure would definitely take me out. But just as he brought his fist a centimetre from my cheek, something pulled him back. Harry! Taking this bad boy down would take a team effort, even if it did sound really cheesy. He was back in his human form, hair blonde as a sunny white beach, and eyes full of hungry rage. Harry wanted to kill the Ticker, there was no doubt. And so did I.

We raged on taking it in turns to trick, punch or kick each other until suddenly, the pendulum flew off the Tickers neck. Except for quite a few grunts and screams, none of us had spoken for a while, but I soon changed that.

"Everything seems to be going our way tonight, isn't it?" I was the closest to the tiny necklace and so I galloped to its side. Harry had The Ticker in a death lock and he wasn't going anywhere, so I figured I could have a little fun. It was cruel, but hey, this guy tried to kill me and Harry. I thought well, why not.

"Poor, poor Ticker. You lost your precious little piece of jewelry, didn't you? Well, it's sort of your own fault, you know. Letting it fall into the wrong hands." Holding it firmly in both of my hands, I pushed it in his face. It was a bit stupid because I found out later; I had cut myself on one of his face metal plates. They burned too, one of his ways to show anger, I guessed. "I guess you'll have to have a little sleepy now, won't you." I teased as I remembered that if you took the pendulum away, he would die for two minutes. Harry let his arms loose and the Ticker fell to the ground. He lay on the floor, gasping for his precious pendulum that was dangling from my hand. A metallic hand was raised up in the air, and then it fell with a dramatic "*thunk*" on to the hard wall. I knew he wasn't dead, of course he couldn't be, but he would be out for a few minutes for us to grab the Arrow and go. Harry was already ahead of me; he flew up to the door and threw down a rope that I hadn't seen before. When I touched it, I realized that it was an elongated monkey's tale and Harry was dangling from the door side and swinging about, clutching on with his weird hairy hands. I grabbed on awkwardly, and could immediately feel little fleas running around between my fingers. Yuck!

Using the wall/floor to balance on, I climbed up to the door and in. As I climbed passed him, he muttered something about being heavy and I playfully kicked his furry little head.

"Hey!"

"It was coming to ya." I explained.

Both of us searched for the Arrow but we couldn't find it anywhere. I was getting really impatient and I almost let loose when Harry started laughing. He leaned against the wall and explained his outburst, "We are such idiots! The Ticker had it, remember? That's why you came down and started beating him up!"

I slapped my forehead hard. Of course! The Ticker was holding it in his hand when I came down, but where had it been while we were fighting. Harry let his tail down and I climbed back to the scene of the fight. I almost screamed when I found the Ticker not where I had left him, but standing on the opposite side of the room, casually leaning against the wall, all his skin grown back. It must have been two minutes while we were stupid enough to forget he had the freaking bronze Arrow. I was not up for another fight, so this one would have to be quick. But I didn't have any fire, I had moronically used up all in one go. Where could I get fire?

"Harry, Dragon!" I yelled before I remember he couldn't do mythical creatures. "Oh yeah." I guessed I was alone on that one, so I charged, screaming at the top of my lungs. Being blown off your feet by the power of wind is quite extraordinary. Harry swooped in as a tiny dragon and puffed a tiny wad of light in front of me. He then retreated to the room above. Without questioning it, I pounced at the fire, making it into a hurricane of flames surrounding the Ticker, but not slim enough to harm him. He couldn't see me creep behind him and grab the Arrow from his back pocket holder thing. Being the brutal person I was, I squashed him in a massive pillar of fire, almost burning him to a crisp. It dispersed as I lost my concentration, focusing only on the Arrow. Harry had flown down beside me and I gave it to him to hold while I inspected the Ticker. I stepped forward, still keeping my distance even though he was smoking and jerking with electric stuff. In a blink, all his clocks and dials turned to zero, and that was the end of the evil time lord, The Ticker.

"Liar," I simply stated.

"What?"

"Dragons are mythical creatures."

"Okay, let me get this straight. You've seen man-eating lava, talking flowers, ghosts, and you still don't think *dragons* are real?"

I couldn't argue with that.

A BROKEN HEART AND AN ESCAPE

We pressed our backs to the wall, as it flipped back to being the floor. Harry had to quickly roll over me so that the dead robot wouldn't squish him as it fell. We stayed lying on our backs for a while, just to catch our breath.

"We got it." I sighed, still panting.

"We made it, we're alive." Harry added.

Simultaneously, we got up and took turns trying to jump up through the trap door to the cupboard. Harry got there first, using kangaroo legs. Everything seemed to be easy to him. It was such a huge power and it seemed that something had gotten into his brain telling him that it was insignificant, even though he used it like a lifestyle. Yet sometimes he refused to morph. If I could be anything I wanted, I would definitely choose to be something other than me and my life. But then again, I'm contradicting myself here; it really did seem to get us out of scrapes an awful lot, especially while we were on the boat. When I read books, the sidekick doesn't usually have a greater power than the hero. So was I really the hero in this story, or am I telling his tale? I was troubled and didn't want to use the rest of my strength to climb up

Harry's tail, but I had to. Harry pulled the string as I got up, closing the door behind me. We stood facing each other in the tiny little room, daring each other to open the door first. We didn't have to. Someone else opened it. Luca. I was so happy to see him; I almost tried to hug him. Another failure resulting in me crashing into the door. Luca gave a flash of a grin, but then got serious.

"What is it?" Something was strange about his face; it was grim and sad, like he just lost his favorite football boots. Well, that's the only thing that came to mind when I saw him, I mean he seemed like a guy who would really like soccer and all, wearing a uniform and spiked boots. I noticed that his ball was missing. I remembered how he'd held it firmly but full of care.

I asked, "Where's your football?" I know I'm pretty forward, but I said it in a pretty caring way I think.

He looked at the floor, "I can't tell you. They'll kill me."

"I thought you were already dead." I blurted out, instantly feeling guilty. He looked so hurt and almost crying.

"Only my body, not my soul." He whispered.

"I thought souls could never die." Harry butted in.

"Mine can. I'm only a plant soul." His voice broke on the word 'plant' and he started balling. To be honest, it was quite awkward seeing a guy my age crying especially since I didn't really understand what he meant, but I could see that he was really, *really* upset. So instead of snickering (which is what I usually do in a weird situation), I tried to comfort him the best I could.

"It's okay. You can tell us anything. I want to help you." I patted his back without going through him. It was awkward comforting air but I had to try.

He pulled himself together, still sniveling though. "You may think I'm a stupid kid crying about losing my ball. But what's inside that soccer ball is so much more important."

"Tell us about it." There didn't seem to be anyone around so I pulled him into the room me and Harry had hidden in before and sat down.

"I was not the only one to have my flower taken by the gypsy. My seeders, my parents, were taken too. When we got here, they didn't like the way Minty Mourners treated people. They rebelled by helping some humans escape and were kept prisoner in a sealed container. I stole it when the ghosts weren't looking and painted it to look like a soccer ball so that I could keep my family with me wherever I go. When the ghosts put two and two together after they saw me helping you, they knew that I must've stolen the container and now they want to punish me. They told me to drown the humans and then I would be able to keep the ball. I'm sorry, I need my parents."

My heart stopped. There was no doubt that I was going to let him drown me. I grew up without my parents being anywhere near me. At least he knew they were there with him. I wasn't going to let him go through my pain. I sent these thoughts to Luca.

"Lead us to the side." As I said this I realized I was giving up my life for his to be happy. It was a huge decision but I made it in a snap second. It was the right choice. I hadn't thought about if Harry would do this with me. I wondered if the Mourners would still give him back his parents if only one human died. Probably not. Not looking back, Luca and I walked to the side of the boat and I prepared to jump.

"Wait!" Harry startled me, so much that I almost fell off. "Maybe we can trick them into thinking that we drowned." I was all for it if it worked out for Luca and we didn't die. I mean, I didn't really want my life to end just before I saved the world. That would have been a bit sad.

"Got any ideas?" Luca sounded hopeful. I climbed down from the side of the railing.

"Yeah. Yeah, a really good one." Harry's smile came from ear to ear. I immediately had complete faith in him.

FAKING DEATH IN FRONT OF GHOSTS

An I idea popped into my mind. "What if Luca got back his ball and came with us. He could live in the Nowhere District! It's not like he's trapped here like the other Mourners." Our smiles brightened.

"After they think you're dead and give me back my mum and dad, I could jump in after you!" Luca chirped in.

"If it's that easy, then why haven't you escaped before?" Harry's brow furrowed and so did mine. How come he always asked the interesting questions before I could?

"I haven't got the nerve. If I'm going with you guys, I think I could do it." He wasn't sure of himself, but I was sure of him.

"Right, so what's the plan, Harry Man." I said in the most kiddy voice I could. I thought a laugh could give Luca some strength.

He was silent. When he realized we were staring at him, he wiggled his eyebrows at us. "Jump and see."

I trusted him, but I didn't understand. Luca didn't say anything either and so me and Harry went back to the cupboard, tied ourselves up and waited as Luca went to fetch the ghost elders.

He told me that he had to jump first to have the plan work and to leave the rest to him. After a few minutes, the door opened and we were let out by big sagging ghosts, their eyes sad but dangerous.

"Come with us." The oldest looking one growled, his voice was really deep. Obediently we followed, after Luca untied us from each other. As we approached the side of the ship, another one spoke in a very high-pitched voice, she looked a bit like Anusha. Maybe she was her mother or something. "Who shall die first?" My hand betrayed my trust in Harry and I decided that I couldn't watch him fall. "You! Boy, you must jump first. To destroy any plans you might have." I saw him suppress a smile as he walked up the step ladder to the railing. I stepped forward to the railing, I didn't know why, it would just make me more upset to watch him fall. Before he jumped, Harry glanced at me and gave a 'thank you' smile, I don't know what for. And then he jumped. Like a professional diver straight into the water. It must have hurt to fall so far. He came up a couple of minutes later to breath and then I watched as he looked like he was being pulled down to the depths.

It was then my turn. I almost ran up the steps, anxious to make sure Harry was okay. Falling felt like flying. Zooming through the air with my hair flapping about by my head. A few metres before I hit the water, everything went black.

I figured I had died quickly, not putting up a fight. But when I woke up, I thought differently. I was in a small, round room, consumed by darkness.

"Alexis, are you okay? You hit the back of my throat pretty hard." A deep version of Harry's voice rang in my ear. I was so confused.

"Uh, where am I?" I asked, disorientated.

"The Minty Mourners think we've both been eaten by a whale, while in actual fact, I am the whale. I caught just before you hit the water. Pretty good plan, eh?"

I didn't even dignify that with an answer. Yes, he was right, but he really could have told me his 'brilliant' plan before I thought I had died.

He continued, "And I didn't tell you because it was important to preserve your acting terrified in front of the ghosts. They won't suspect a thing. Ow!"

"What?" He had screamed and I jumped up, "Did they figure it out? They're coming after us, aren't they? Oh no, oh no, oh no!" I pictured the giant boat smashing into the miniature whale and Harry switching and shifting into different things, with me inside of him. I lay down on the floor in a hopeless pile.

"No! The Deafeners are screeching!" He suddenly picked up speed and I was almost thrown off his tongue and down his throat.

"Woah there, speedy." We slowed down after a while and washed up on the beach. Harry slowly opened his giant mouth and I simply stepped out of the enormous whale. He changed back to normal Harry before I could turn around and watch. He gave off a flash of pain as he slogged over to me. We made a silent decision to sit down and wait for Luca.

We waited until dawn, not sleeping a wink, wanting to

see the happiness on Luca's face when he reached safety away from the boat. We waited and waited. When no one came, Harry wanted to give up, but I was going to stay there until I saw his face again. I felt responsible for his soul and his life, and wanted to pay him back for helping us move a step closer to our destination. Sadness filled my heart when I realized I hadn't seen his smile as much as I should have. I swore that I would make his life better, then and there.

But I couldn't. Though I didn't know it at that point, Luca was dead and soulless.

PAPER THIN

A flat, grey, paper thin sheet lay on top of the waves. As it moved closer, I could make out a curved body shape and I knew that Luca was gone. His beautiful soul washed up beside where I was crouching. He was smiling his hands by his side, the way I would have wanted to see him all the time. I reached out; fingers outstretched, and tried to hold his hand. But as soon as I came near his dead ghost, it disappeared into thin air. Harry kneeled beside me and we sat together, it was almost like we were waiting for him to come back. Be a double-dead soul or something.

"*He's gone.*" We had been silent for a while, but a voice inside me broke my personal silence. It must have been the same voice that had spoken to me on the volcano that night. "*He's gone and there is nothing you can do about it.*"

There is one thing, I thought, as I saw a small globe like thing floating in the water.

I waded out to Luca's parents and held them close in my arms, not letting Harry come near them. Without looking back, I dived back through the hole and came up in warm darkness, since it was night in the Nowhere District, still clutching Luca's parent's souls.

I heard Harry splash up behind me.

"There's an empty patch over there." Harry knew what I was planning to do. Luca's parents fought for freedom and so they had to be buried in freedom. Outside of that terrible place.

The soil was soft in the place Harry had pointed to, so I just dug with my hands and he gently placed the sphere inside the deep hole. We padded the mud back into place together, then sat back and watched. I think we were hoping that somehow, out of magic, Luca and his parents would sprout out of the ground once more, being reborn into their home.

It was kind of like a funeral; the Singers hummed a sad melody and Harry and I talked about Luca, imagining what type of flower he was, what we would have done if he had made it to us.

I cried for the very first time in my life that day. And Harry was there to help me through it.

MOVING ON AND AWKWARD SONGS

At about sundown the next day, we left the burial site to venture towards our next destination. I had cried myself to sleep that night, not just because of Luca but because of everything. I remembered all the things that had made me want to weep in the past; my parents, the hard work I was pushed to do by Lola, a boy a long time ago, and most recently, GG.

What happened with the boy was this; I had a crush on this guy called Arne. Some girl told him about it and he beat me up. Badly. I was in hospital for nearly a week. Not that he cared. He got off easy, since it was the first time he had been *caught* doing it, he got a warning and had to pay the bills. They didn't even try to make him say sorry; he wasn't that sort of guy. I remembered the pain it had caused me, physically and emotionally. I swore an oath that day, never to show how I felt to anyone but myself. Crying in front of Harry, even though he was very comforting, made me feel ashamed to have broken my oath, but then also relieved me of the heavy weight of bottled up emotions I had carried around with me every single day of my life.

We walked in silence for a few hours, had a quick

lunch, and then ran on a sugar high the whole way to the Hidden Door. Harry plunked down in front of it and decided for both of us to have a nap in the warm daylight.

The Singers hummed soft tunes of familiar songs. But then, the one closest to Harry sang a peculiar song I had never heard before. It went something like this:

> *As the waves slide up,*
> *The ghost and the girl,*
> *Are close and happy,*
> *While the boy,*
> *Sits alone and shameful.*
> *But as the dawn approaches*
> *And the ship beckons,*
> *The soul must retreat,*
> *Leaving the darling heartbroken*
> *And in need of love,*
> *The boy comes to rescue,*
> *Yet she pushes him away,*
> *For her love for the Mourner*
> *Is set in stone.*

It was an odd song and I couldn't make sense of it. I mean, I knew it had to do with Luca, but...

Singers read minds, so they must've read Harry's dream. I shook him awake quickly so that I wouldn't have to listen to another word of it. Was Harry jealous that I was really upset when Luca died? That would mean that Harry wanted me all to himself. I was confused and didn't know what to say. I let Harry do the talking.

"What the heck? I was dreaming!" He yelled. As soon as he woke up, the flower went back to its normal hum.

"I know," slipped out.

"Excuse me?"

"Nothing."

There was a silence between us and we didn't meet each other's eyes. Soon, we both fell asleep, although my nap was restless. It wasn't that I was thinking of anything in particular, it was just that I couldn't get comfortable and the sun was glaring at me. I didn't know what it was, but it felt like my instincts were going crazy, like something big was about to happen. Harry kept kicking me in his sleep, probably chasing a rabbit or something.

I finally gave up trying to sleep and thought about his dream song. Why did he think I was in love with Luca? I didn't believe in that sort of thing. Sure, I liked him and I don't want anyone to die, but it wasn't *like that*. Ugh, my brain wouldn't stop thinking about it. I decided to just drop it and tried to fall asleep once again, failing.

FIREWORKS

The winds blew to and fro through the cool night, outside the wide open Hidden door. It must have been a different one we had been through before, even though it looked very similar. It was dark in both lands but through the doorway was a different world. A desert; the Doomful Desert. I was surprised because you would expect a vast land of sun and heat, to be, well, hot. I guess the sun had to go away at some point. Harry walked through first, out of the beautiful giant flower garden and into an even emptier place.

"We should probably read the section." Harry said gloomily.

"Yeah, I guess," I pulled out the book as I stepped through the door, "Doomful Desert- A land of hate and heat, where you are against yourself and your own state of mind. It deceives you in many ways; quick sand, mirages and the scorcher. Wet quick sand will drown you in waves of heat." Harry's face went pale. "The Scorcher- the sun in the desert is no ordinary sun. The wanderer will find that after a few hours in the perpetual heat, their skin slowly becomes the opposite to frost bite; boil bite.

His face went a dull shade of pale white. "This is the last one. Fox Flies: In the Doomful Desert live these creatures of deception. They hide themselves, camouflaged in the sand dunes, and await their prey. When the victim gets too close, the bugs send mirages into the unfortunate's mind, of their most wanted desire, which is usually, at that point in the desert, as oasis, overflowing with water. The thirsty traveler's hopes rise, only to be crushed by the taste of salty sand as they lean into take a sip of the inviting and glistening water. Their mind is lost after many repetitions of this charade. Lost in the soft sands forever. The only way to defeat these dragonfly- like terrors is to kill them with your mind, be smarter than them, pretend to fall for their nasty tricks, and then crush their hopes for every time you do not fall as a slave to them, insane."

He fainted. I wasn't worried, but the fact that he hadn't keeled over from listening to the other descriptions before confused me. A thought sprang to mind that he might not like the idea of the mind manipulating aspect. I had an idea. Digging around in my backpack I pulled out my matchbox just as Harry came to.

"W-What are you doing?" He sounded nervous.

"Relax, it's a surprise." I said with an evil grin. Closing the door behind me, and flicking a light, I stored up all my energy/chi into that little flame.

"Woah, what are you doing?" He sounded really worried now, what he didn't trust me? I didn't blame him. Bringing all my energy to the surface, I shaped the fire into a rocket. Now, for the finale. I let it burst into the cool night air, exploding right next to the beautiful full moon. The fireworks made a faint H shape and I saw Harry's face light up with surprise and pleasure.

I shot up a few more, making the lights into different shapes. An A for me, Alexis, a flame (also for me) and an odd shape that I planned to be a dog, but sort of turned out to be a really lumpy snake thing. I sat next to him on the dry sand looking up at bright stars. Living in a town, you hardly ever saw stars because of the lights on the ground. Harry pointed out all the star signs and pictures. The sky was completely clear of clouds and the moon was amazing.

SAND, SAND AND MORE SAND

"What is with you and the fox flies?" I could feel him flinch and tense up beside me.

"Well, the whole 'using your own mind against you' thing. I've never been too good with my emotions, feelings or thoughts, you know, ever since that day…" His voice walked off into the silence and I had no idea what to say in response. I couldn't agree with him, I mean, like I said a while ago, I didn't usually show off my emotions that much.

So I just nodded and rolled over so my back was facing him. The conversation was taking an awkward turn. I completely believed that he couldn't control his emotions. The dream was still bugging me.

"There's Orion's Belt. It's simple but definitely my favorite." I followed his finger to each of the stars that shone like diamonds. I kept my mouth shut.

Harry sighed loudly and I think he fell asleep after a few minutes. I, on the other hand, couldn't help but be uncomfortable. The sand and bugs kept going into my ear and the ground was too flat to lie straight on. I wriggled about, rubbing my ear to get anything out.

"Shoulder." Harry said, dreamily.

"Huh?"

"Rest on your shoulder. A desert tribe I read about would sleep on the sand and rest their heads on their shoulders with their elbow supporting it. I bet it wasn't very comfortable, but it was their trick to keep the critters out."

I tried his idea and yes, my arm and neck hurt for the most part of night, but I still got a little slip of sleep in there somewhere.

When morning came, Harry was already up and cooking. Cooking, as in making sandwiches with toasted ham. Toasted, because the sun had burnt them while he buttered the bread. It was boiling and only dawn. As soon as my eyes were able to open, I shut them faster than a bullet fired at close range. The Scorcher was so bright that I had to put on two pairs of sunglasses before I could even squint. Harry had done the same. I practically tore my shirt off (don't worry I had a singlet on underneath) and ran behind Harry to throw on some really short shorts.

"I wouldn't do that if I were you," he yelled as he turned around and ran towards me. I noticed he was wearing a hoodie and trousers.

"Aren't you boiling?" I screamed, the wind was picking up and loud.

"Of course I am, idiot. But I don't want to get sunburned or worse." I remember that worse was the complete opposite of frost bite, boil bite, and I ran to my bag to throw on all my clothes. I even managed to find a balaclava and put that on. When I had finished pulling on the outfits, I swore I would die of heat stroke within one kilometre of walking. Possibly one metre. And I had to carry a backpack.

"How do I look?" I raised my puffy arms; my voice was muffled by the tight fitting mask.

"Um….hot." I just looked at him.

He stuttered, "I-I mean, hot as in temperature hot, like heat hot. Not hot i-in… that way."

"Thanks." I said sarcastically, but when I turned around I smiled. He was nervous around me. That meant I had power over him. Oh great, I was becoming a psychopathic power freak in the desert.

So the hours went by. And so did the days. Every second was a living hell; in fact, it would have been the most generous gift to die at some points. But on the ninth day, we made a camp that we would live in for a while. You know, catch our breath after what we had done. Harry and I put up a make shift tent by breaking our hiking sticks in half and using them as poles, and stitching various pieces of clothing together for a roof. Stitching as in using duct tape. Lots of duct tape. It wasn't much of a house (or even a tent) but it at least reduced the glare a bit. We spent three weeks in that little hovel thing.

Until it came. The sand storm.

It started off with a low whistle, and the sand beneath our feet started to shift and reshape. There were mounds of sand all around us, so couldn't see very far, but then, one by one, the little mountains began to shake and disappear into the wind. The wind that was coming towards us. We had definitely not planned for that, even though we knew it was a possibility. Harry was hyperventilating and I was close to panicking as well. What stories had I heard about sand storms? Oh, I couldn't remember. I figured it was a death trap, if we breathed in that giant sand tsunami, it would go into our lungs and... well, I wasn't much of a doctor. It rushed and rolled towards us like a vertical hurricane.

And then it hit us, throwing me right off my feet. Thankfully, we had salvaged most of our belongings in our bags before it got to us, yet much was lost. Though my eyes were tightly shut and stingy with agony, I could sense Harry spinning out of control beside me.

The taste of burning hot salt filled my mouth and I couldn't breathe without it going up my nose. It was sick and salty and I can't explain how awful it was. Imagine spinning around in a giant washing machine, except it's not water, but burning hot sand. I never want to go to the beach again after that.

A small lizard brushed past my face and I tried very hard to suppress a girlish squeal as it tried to cling onto my eyebrows with its sticky little reptilian hands.

I felt Harry lunge at my hand and grab onto it for dear life, not that it would help very much. But I held on to his as well. There we were, flying through the air and holding hands. It wasn't awkward at the time, because you know, we were about to die. We were just terrified and glad to have someone to die with. We had nothing to lose. And everything was lost in the scolding, golden sands of the Doomful Desert.

CAPTURED BY THE WIND

Do you sometimes wish that you could crawl into a small hole and stay there for the rest of your life, never wanting to see another soul again, hiding from the terribly cruel world? Well, that's where we were stuck. In a small cavity of air underneath a massive pile of, you guessed it, freakin' sand. We had been unconscious for I don't know how long, but I guessed not too long, otherwise we would have already run out of air. Harry was still lulling in and out of consciousness when I raised my hand to paw through the sand. A tiny voice, that I could barely hear came from within me, *it'll all pile on you if you go from the top, not the best decision.* My grandfather was smart, unlike me, who almost suffocated us even more.

How were we going to get out of this? I had no idea. A few scenarios came to mind of Harry turning into 'sand' animals and crawling out of the crevice giving me more air to survive a bit longer. But then what would happen after a bit longer. I would eventually breath in all the oxygen left and slowly suffocate. Unless Harry had a better plan. I carefully shook him awake, trying not to use up too much energy. If we talked we would use up lots more air (I was being seriously careful) so I started fingering the sand and wrote: "Got anything?"

He rubbed what I had written and replied. "I think so, but you're not going to like it."

"What is it?"

"Well, it's not much of a plan to save us, but…"

"Yes, yes, go on." I interrupted.

"Well, maybe I should be a snake and slither up to see how far we are from the surface."

I didn't write for a while and thought what he wrote through. Then I realized something.

"We can't be that far, because we wouldn't be able to see underground! Oh my gosh, we are so stupid. We're probably only a few centimetres from the surface." Harry started to respond, but I didn't pay attention and started to paw my way up through the sand. I spoke this time. "Harry, I can make a hole for me but I'm going to need to put the sand somewhere in here." He understood and I heard him slithering away into the sand. As I clawed away, I noticed I couldn't breathe. *Oh gosh,* I thought. In a really hoarse voice, I yelled, "Harry! Anytime soon would be good!" After digging for about half a minute, my hand escaped the sweaty sand, to a hotter environment in the sun.

I was stuck. I couldn't use up any more air. I waited and waited, for Harry to pull me out into the beam of the Scorcher. I felt so useless, so helpless. It was such a cliché that I was so close to the surface, yet so far from surviving.

And slowly, I took in my last sip of air and let it out as the darkness came in.

LOST AND HUNGRY

In my haze of suffocation and heat stroke, I felt a hand pull me out into the desert. I lay still, gulping big mouthfuls of air that tasted like salt. The silhouette against the sun, fed me warm water which I slurped greedily, almost choking to death. After a long drink, lying back down on the re-formed sand, I remembered another time when I lay in the blazing sun of the Nowhere District. It felt like months since we first entered that haven of music. Well, it had been months. I counted up the days we had traveled on my calendar (I had kept a clear note of each day so that we wouldn't lose track of time and go crazy), remembering each moment vividly. Eighty four days we had been away from home, almost three months.

Yet, I didn't really miss anyone, except maybe Bernie whose pies and pastries were amazing (I've said this before, I just thought I should emphasize it because they really are true bliss). I thought about the normal days I would spend wasting away on that horrible training course with Lola criticizing my every move. A smile came to me when I remembered how she would caress her AK47 as she told her story of disarming a whole SWAT team of enemies and keeping it as her prize. I think she even named it, Sergeant Melore, after her right hand man who she lost in combat. The nights I would spend hours and hours tearing through every census ever taken and recorded in our country looking for anyone living by the name of Blake, yet finding nothing. And then the night the man from Social Services came to my door and told me that GG was out there, found, and Lola made arrangements for the next day. The day that changed my life for eternity.

"You okay?" Harry's rusty voice was even more croaky with his sore throat. He was standing over me, water bottle in hand and looking out at the surrounding sand.

I tried to reply but all that came out was a sound that could only resemble a toad with really bad period pains. I sat up and nodded, hugging my knees to hide my pained expression because I sat up too fast (if I were in a cartoon, I would have little stars floating around my head). He pulled me up to my feet and I realized what he had been staring at. The whole desert had taken on a different shape than before. We stood at the top of a hill overlooking a golden valley that stretched for millions of acres. We had been travelling north the whole time so I figured, since we couldn't tell which direction we had come from by eye, my compass would point us right. But when I took it out of my sandy bag, (I was really, really surprised to still have it on my back) it flickered and jumped to all different points not sitting still for a second. I showed it to Harry and he studied it for a very long time, trying to see if one point was the most frequently passed. He finally decided it was west- north - west, though I doubted its accuracy.

"Come on, honey, don't be a typical man. Why don't we just ask for directions?" I mimicked an old couple I had heard on the radio a few years before.

"I see you haven't lost your sparkling sense of humor, Miss Blake," He sounded cross, I presumed at the compass, "but I don't think it'll be very helpful here."

"I'm sorry, Mr. Sensitive," I said and started walking in the direction he pointed. I was completely flabbergasted (that's right, I do use awesome words like that) at how different the world around us looked. It was like I had dived into the sand bank and gone through to a different place. The blue sky seemed more sinister, like the baby shade was too sweet. And the fields below our feet seemed to glow more glimmering golden every second. Every second turned into every minute and every minute into every hour. Then into every day. And then we were somehow descending into another week of endless trudging through the desert.

As we sat down for another quickie meal of sandwiches (I was beginning to be surprised at how long peanut butter could last) Harry pulled out the ingredients.

The bread was moldy and stale. Something had gotten into the Oreos. And almost all our other supplies had disappeared. Probably down our gullet's but we were still in shock.

"What happened to our provisions?!" I nearly screamed.

Neither of us responded. It looked like we were going to be running low for a while. My tummy rumbled like a thunder cloud on the horizon. Speaking of which, there was a cloud on the horizon. A great, big one.

DISAPPOINTMENT

As the storm rolled towards us, I realized with dread that this experience wasn't in the book. Slowly and steadily, I scrunched around in my bag to fish it out. Flicking through the old pages frantically, I scanned the Desert Sections once again but found nothing about a rain storm. Just my luck.

"Harry, what do we do?" I actually sounded terrified, so much for keeping my emotions in check. But I couldn't deal with it anymore. Just the thought of coming all this way to be washed away or sucked into wet quick sand, at the last minute, was unthinkable. I grabbed his arm and shook it hard when he didn't answer. His head slowly turned to me and I had no idea what to the think. His expression was one of sheer delight. "Uh, Harry. What?"

"Everything is fine. We're saved." His eyes seemed to be glazed over and staring into the distance, right into the center of the storm.

"No! No, Harry we're not saved. We're hardly close to surviving, okay. There is a huge Cumulonimbus heading right towards us in the middle of the desert where there is no cover, and remember what the book said? If the sand gets wet, it turns to quick sand which, as the name suggests, can sink us pretty quickly!" I nearly screamed the last sentence. What was he thinking?

In the distance behind us, I saw tiny little bugs hovering in the air watching us. The Fox Flies. He must have been seeing them, their delusions I mean.

"Harry, what do you see?" I gave off a gentler tone, but stern so that he would answer fast.

"I see...a mountain...and a cave...the Carnivorous Cave...our next destination."A gentle vision of relief spread across his face and it took all my strength to fight through the happiness he was feeling and ignore the little voice inside my head telling me to keep that smile on his face. "Harry. Listen to me, there is no cave. Okay, none of that is real. It's just your mind playing tricks on you, you have to fight past it!" I urged him, I started to feel hopeless, "Come on, Harry. You can do this. Just think of all the real things in your life think of all the scary and amazing things you've been through. You were so lucky to meet GG when you were in need. But this, right now, it isn't luck. This is fantasy. It's tragic but we have to push past it."

His eyes flickered and he lost his balance for a second, I thought *yes! He's back to normal.* But as soon as he regained a steady stand, his arms flew in front of him reaching for the 'cave' murmuring something unrecognizable. Harry took a slow step forward. I grabbed his shoulders in a final act of desperation but he just shook me off like a jacket. I kneeled down on the ground losing all hope.

As the storm moved closer, I could make out the

bucketing rain in the distance and it hit me. Rain in the desert? It was hardly possible, and a cloud this big. And so much water! "It's going to be okay!" I yelled to no one in particular. Harry walked on to the so called cave that he saw. With my new burst of excitement, I jumped up just as he was reaching out. "Harry, don't! It's not real." As I ran towards him, I could no longer feel the sun on my back. The cloud was right above me when I looked up. A screech of joy escaped me and ran even faster. I even managed a cartwheel in there. I quickly grabbed the back of his ripped up shirt and threw him to the ground. I lay with him with my tongue outstretched, waiting for the refreshing cool rain.

But it never came. I waited and waited for the succulent liquid, yet there was none. Even when the sun came back into view and the light burned my pupils, I wouldn't accept it. Even when Harry told me I had been tricked by the evil Flies I didn't budge. Finally, he got impatient and threw me over his shoulder. I hadn't realized he was that strong, but I didn't notice at the time, still in a haze of disbelief and self-pity. I closed my eyes and let everything overpower me.

OUR FIRST MEETING

A blur that vaguely resembled a tall man stood over me. I tried to speak but all that came out was a muffled cough. I was gagged.

"Hello there, you must be Miss Alexis Blake. I hope you had a pleasant journey, although it was for absolutely nothing." The silhouette above me spoke in a tart and squeaky voice. He stood with arms crossed over his chest leaning against a wall. "I hope this isn't too painful, but I do love to watch people scream." He walked slowly towards me, and whispered the end of his sentence. His icy breath made me shiver and jump. It had felt like a small pump of electricity went through my brain. As my eyes adjusted to the dark, I could make out a smooth childish face with an extremely pointy nose. There was no sign of a single hair on his shiny head but there was a long deep scar that wound around his whole head like a band. He was dressed in a pinstriped suit and bright red gloves. He pulled and slapped one onto his hand with a loud thwack and smiled menacingly displaying his golden and yellow teeth.

"The name is Zacheri Smoke. Pleasure to meet you."

Zacheri Smoke held out his large, ungloved hand with unusually long fingers for me to shake. Even if I wanted to shake his evil hand, I wouldn't have been able to since my hands were strapped behind my back around a pole of some sort. I saw my feet were tied too. "Oh yes, I'm sorry," he didn't sound sincere at all, "you're all tied up. It's so that you don't run off while we have a little…chat."

Do you ever get the feeling that you just want to punch the person you're with right in the face? Guess what. I had that feeling, except on a much bigger scale. I wanted to kill him. Even if I didn't know who he really was or what he did, his growly, vicious voice could have ticked any normal person off. He was such a…jerk.

"So you'll probably want an explanation right now. Hmm, What was that? I can't hear you, sweetheart, you're gagged!" He chuckled at his own joke and glared at his new henchmen to laugh also. Some deep voices laughed all too enthusiastically. He continued, "Your 'boyfriend' is dead. He tried to carry you up the wall to the cave entrance but as soon as he got here, I was waiting." The evil man pulls out a 62 Caliber gun and points it right at my forehead and then to my heart. "Bang and bang. He's behind you if you'd like to pay your respects." Some big burly hands grabbed my wrists and yanked me up into a standing position. Hot tears of fury stained my face as my head was turned for me to look at Harry's limp body on the floor, in a puddle of blood. A sob escaped me, it was the worst thing I could have done because it showed Smoke that I was weak. Harry's eyes were still open, looking up at the ceiling like it was the night sky. The rough hands behind me undid my hand restraints and I half hopped, half ran to Harry's side. Not caring about the bloody mess, dove next to him and shook him. I knew it wouldn't work to bring him back to life. But I had to try. Every ounce of me longed for him, needed him; he couldn't die or I would. At that moment, I realized how much I loved him. He had been with me the whole time, helping me through, encouraging me to go on. He was my best and only friend in this race. And I needed him more than ever.

The henchman stepped back calmly, just far enough that he wouldn't see me carefully untie my feet restraints, as it looked like I was just hugging my knees and watching his dead body. Wiping away the tears was actually a disguise for tearing off the tape on my mouth and wobbly standing up by clutching the wall was me taking a solid hunk of it out. In one swift movement, I flung the rock right at the burly man's face. All those years of training paid off in the next ten minutes. As the first guy plummeted down to the ground a second came charging. His face was round like a globe and covered in gory tattoos of war scenes. He carried a long axe that could cut right through anyone in a single swish. Before he swung his heavy blade I twisted under and threw a round house kick right into his back. That one I had learnt on my own from days at an endlessly boring middle school. He recovered quite quickly and stepped forward for a stabbing attack. I scooted back but not quick enough because I felt a sharp pain in my abdomen but ignored it hoping it was just a scratch. As I was distracted by a movement from the rock guy, the axe guy threw a punch at my nose, certainly fracturing it.

My only counter attack to that one was some very colorful language. He swiped at my leg making me fall right on my bum. Scuffling back to the wall, I sprung up. The rock guy came at me and threw another punch at my face but I fall back at the last second so that he punched the wall so hard that I could hear a horrible crackling sound coming from his fist. He collapsed, caressing his broken hand. A few kicks to the head finished him off. I felt a burning fire in my heart, scorching any conscience I might have had. I took another swipe to the head that broke his neck immediately.

With my heart still racing dangerously fast, I plunged at the henchman holding the axe and quickly karate chopped his hand losing the axe before he realized I was coming at him. With a mighty low kick *thwack!* he lost his manhood forever. He leaned forward clutching his crotch as I knee-ed him right in the face, breaking his nose as well as some teeth. He grabbed his face and I kicked him in his stomach a few times, until he too collapsed in pain.

It all felt too easy, even though I had some pretty nasty scars. It's not all the time that a fourteen year old girl gets to take out two heavy set guys, one of whom has a weapon.

I HAVE SOME TALENT

A slow clap came from behind me. I had forgotten about the man that currently wanted to kill me.

He chuckled, "Well done, Miss Blake. I see you have some talent. But now it's my turn." His continuous grin bugged me, but he didn't deserve to see my anger over such a little thing. So I smiled back and he ranted on, "Over here I have two boxes. One is a battery, my weapon. The other is a box of matches, your weapon. Do you understand?"

I nodded curtly. "They're pretty much the same." I had a little something up my sleeve.

"How do you mean? Our powers?" I saw a tiny hint of confusion behind his plastered mask of evil happiness.

"Well, I can do this;" I expertly pulled a match from the box and lit it, then powered flames onto the unconscious bodies of his henchmen, "and you can burn things with your electricity. Either way, at the end of this, we'll both have some pretty bad scorch marks."

He gave me a quizzical look, then it became thoughtful, but slowly the evil crooked grin reappeared, and he beamed at me with his burning eyes. As fast as the speed of light, I was on the floor writhing in pain. He had used all ten of his electric volts on me at his first move. I was paralyzed from the waist down and the smell of singed hair filled the room. I had not been expecting that. It was time to give him a piece of my mind. Since his men were still engulfed in flames, I threw both of the fire packages right at Smoke.

Zacheri stepped slowly out from between the blazing bodies and grinned once more with red fury in his eyes. His suit was shredded and singed, the trousers almost completely burnt off up to his knees. His skin was covered in red blotches and welts, some of them oozing with disgusting yellow pus already.

As the numbness wore off, I hastily inspected myself. My hair was like a mane surrounding my head; It had grown out to a heavy length since I left home, my skin; red raw, and stinging like crazy all over.

The longer we stared at each other, our bodies askew and messed up with injuries, the more I hated him. Although it was impossible to despise someone past wanting to rip them apart, deep in my heart, there was a yearning for him to feel pain, such pain that would lead him to insanity. To destroy everything he was and ever will be in the history books to come.

I raised my arm in false surrender, while prying at my legs to move, or even just stretch. "Okay. I give up. You win. Spare me, please." Dropping the sarcasm, true anguish came to my red face as the feeling of dread really sank in. What if my legs really weren't ever going to move again? I thought about this for minute. And then I dropped the trick altogether and the real begging started, "Please, have mercy. I'll give up and go home I swear. Just help me walk again." The tears started to run through the plastered blood of my broken nose and drip down off my chin. There was no mercy to be found in his eyes.

"I am surprised, Ms. Blake. I thought you would be full of rage by now. Your Harry is dead. Your Grandmother is most probably dead. The world will come under my power once I get to the Ice Empress. And you are going to die in approximately five minutes."

Questions swirled around inside my mind. A croaky voice from deep in my throat said "My Grandmother is *most probably* dead? You mean you didn't take her?"

"Yes. Reasonable thing to do for me, really. If I had taken her, it would have set you back and possibly stopped you from completing your journey. She could've also given me leverage. But no, I did not take your precious GG from you. I do know the people who took her though. One of my best men, the one you killed in the volcano blast, was spying on you for a while. Checking out how you functioned. Thank you for disposing of him by the way; he wasn't the brightest of the bunch." On the word 'bunch', his eyes quickly flicked sideways with a short jolt and a giant heap of man grabbed me by the hair and swung his fist into my temple, pushing me right into the haze of unconsciousness.

SHOWDOWN, BOLTS AND BAT-ERIES

When my eyes fluttered open again, Zacheri and his yet more henchman were sitting at a table, sipping from small clay cups. Everything was getting so confusing. How was all this possible?

"She has awoken," the burly man muttered, "May I dispose of her now?"

His squeaky voice replied, "No, I haven't finished my part yet." He turned to me as he slugged down the rest of his drink. I presumed it was alcohol, or some strong drink. His eyes were blood shot and his many patches of burnt skin were sagging and probably still searing. I turned my head to see Harry's body limply hanging from a noose in front of the exit of the cave. I inspected myself, still feeling jolted and jumpy, and still with the electrified to a crisp pain. At least my hair wasn't as big as it was before.

I too, had a rope around my neck, but was standing on a small red clay stool. I could see it was a little off balance, so I didn't dare move an inch. I figure there was a wall behind me; otherwise I wouldn't have been able to sleep standing up. "So Miss Blake, you have awakened yet again. Lucky you, I was just about to settle my knife into your heart. But I guess it's more honorable to look you in the eye when doing the job, isn't it," he snarled.

I opened my mouth to speak but found that it was almost glued shut with dry blood from my ever-pouring nose. I swore under my breath as the glistening stream sprinkled down my clothes and onto the floor, leaving a small pool of red. My cracked throat managed to salvage the little saliva it had left to spit on Zacheri's oily shoes. But it was a pathetic gesture and only made me look even weaker in his merciless hand.

"Ah, I see you are thirsty! Here, have a little something to drink." He flicked his fingers and Angus, as I later found out was his name, silently pulled up the table they had been sitting at. The jug and three cups of whatever it was stood on it. Zacheri picked up the untouched cup and pressed it towards me, mockingly. My fingers reached up to the cup, warily and desperately at the same time. My need won me over and I slurped down the burning liquid. It must have been some poison; it burnt the back of my throat like had swallowed a bee. Yet it gave a friendly tingling sensation and warmth that I have to admit I quite liked. I reached for more, but the Smoke pulled the glass away faster than I expected and I tumbled towards him.

The noose caught me quick short and for a moment I was a sure goner. But the hulk of a man rested the stool right under my feet before my whole weight came to hang by my neck to break it. Zacheri slowly returned to the table and poured another glass for him and his goon.

I was feeling useless. What had my fire powers done to help my case in the past months? Almost nothing, that's what. Looking back, I felt that Harry had done most of the work. And he was out of my reach at that moment in time. Gone, I thought, forever.

Another volt shot me awake from my despairing daydream and I lifted my head up again to the horrible face that was my arch enemy. The despair and sadness slowly melted away and in its place came a raging pit of fire, full of anger and hate, desperate for Zacheri Smoke to plunge into its depths. Was he torturing me? What information did he want, what could I possibly give him? Or was it just the pleasure of hurting his competition and the victory of winning. Yep, I went with that.

"Are you quite finished, sir?" I gagged and spat blood out of my red crisp lips.

He walked slowly towards me with his elongated fingers outstretched, what had the book said about those fingers, I recited it in mind, *"Zacheri Smoke's fingers are longer than any human's because they are electric guns that shoot out bolts of painful electricity,"* Oh great, that is so perfectly peachy.

"I am beginning to get tired of this incessant winning of mine," Zacheri purred after he had pushed about ten more shots of electricity through my side, back and legs. Lola had taught me how to withstand pain during torture and I had been pretty good at it. But no amount of practice or training could prepare anyone for this. I was shaking from head to toe with shear agony. It felt like I had swum across the ocean and hadn't breathed the whole way, with a swarm of jellyfish at my side. I could barely hold my body up straight and had resorted to clutching on to the noose rope. Soon my hands would give way also and I would fall to the terrifying consequence of the snaking slug around my neck. "So let's make this interesting, Miss Blake." And then, with muffled words that seemed to be in a different language, he spoke to the dark corner behind me. As he did so, Angus pulled off my rope and I slumped with a loud thunk down to the floor. I lay there, completely out of energy and very close to passing out once again.

The buzzing noise grew louder and louder. I must have hit my head really hard. "What....what is that?" I mumbled helplessly.

"These are Bat-eries, you should know what they are, right? 'Miniature, electric bats surround the dark Zacheri Smoke, sort of like his henchmen. They send little shockwaves of insanity through the brain that only last for about 10 seconds and then they have to recharge for 5 minutes. Can be fatal to those who don't believe in the impossible. A wide imagination can overpower one if it chooses the right moment.' So let's see how wide your imagination is, Ms Blake." He mocked and chuckled. I was sure I had heard that explanation before. Yes! Of course, that was how Harry explained them to me!

"H-how did you know to-"

"To explain it like that? Oh, a friend of a friend told me that was how it was being told throughout Zoal." He smiled without his teeth, like he knew something that I didn't. This made me very angry.

I attempted to seem aggressive, "Who? W-what are

you saying?" but I failed miserably. I sounded like a moaning sick cat.

"Poor, poor little girl. You are so sad to look at, you know." He towered over me and I tried to kick his leg with impish power.

This was it. I had given up. There was no hope for me against this man with terrifying power who could crush me with a small movement at any time. I burrowed my face in the earth and felt like moving over next to Harry, but I had lost my bearings and had no power to move an inch. Not until Angus pulled me up onto my feet. Before I could fall back down, he set one of the clay stools under me.

"So, Miss Blake. I have to say you have been deceived, Harry was wrong. My bat-eries do not shoot insanity through your brain, but fear. Hallucinations of your worst enemies and fears are against you in your mind. In fact, your imagination is against you. The bigger it is, the more your fears become real." And then he laughed the most stereotypical laugh of a super villain.

He placed another box of matches in my hand as he arranged his flying henchmen. They hovered in the air as Smoke moved them into an orderly line from the smallest to the largest, the smallest being at the front. I fumbled with one of the matches, trying to set it alight before he finished his little 'OCD' ritual. When a small flame finally came about, it was too late. He was ready and waiting. My heart was beating, but it wasn't going at a sure pace, it seemed to falter with fear every now and then. The flame blew out and Zacheri calmly waited as I shakily pulled out a new match. That one also faded out. On my fourth or fifth try, I managed to sustain a hearty glow, but I had to protect it with my arm so that the wind from outside wouldn't blow it out. As I felt the fire inside of me grow, I let out the gulp of air I had been holding in and, instead of blowing it out, the fire grew large. I immediately forced it at Zacheri, pushing it with all my inner strength. But it was no use. Through my flames came the first batch of the bat-eries, the smallest ones.

Pictures flashed behind my eyelids of the horrors I never ever wanted to see. My head buzzed and brain screamed at me to stop thinking of the pictures, to just push them aside. The images of horrifying fears that I've always had ever since I was a child just kept coming. So the first batch must have been just your imaginary fears, the ones that are not possible, but still terrify you. No matter how much I have ever tried, those fears will never go away.

Just when I thought this round had died down, it came back worse than before. Much worse. I saw murky waters that had hidden creatures lurking under the surface, only their glowing eyes visible and their sharp teeth shining, of doctors with hundreds of medicines strapped around their lab coats, searching for a pathetic soul to test their concoctions on. My eyes opened, and for a brief moment, Zacheri was one of those doctors, staring at me hungrily and grinning with his gold and silver dentures. I let out a short scream of sheer terror and disbelief. But when I blinked he was back. I plucked the stingers out of my arm and chest slowly, holding in my squeals and screams for later.

I decided on a strategy for the next section of bateries. I put the match in my mouth and instead of breathing the fire at the bugs, I ducked down just as they were coming at my face and shot the fire right at Smoke's legs. He jumped back and yelped, the bugs hit the wall hard and I leapt right back up again.

But the stupid mistake of trying this war strategy twice got me in a whole load of trouble. As I knelt down on the ground, the bats made a quick waterfall move right on top of my head, attacking my neck and face.

Everything went blurry and every noise around me was muffled like the water dripping in the deeper cave and the scrapping of feet on the clay floor, and my own screams. In my haze I saw a man and a women standing in front of me as I cowered on the floor. Their features were scattered and distorted, almost disgusted. "H-help me. Please, please help me!" My voice echoed in my own ears. I only realized who the two figures were as they faded away into nothing and I screamed in anguish. I covered my face with my fingers but soon they were ripped off and slammed on the ground. GG knelt beside me and appeared to be shouting but I couldn't hear anything. Her face was disappointed. I begged her not to leave me, I pulled at her and wanted to hold on to her forever. But she stood up, easily pealing my pleading hands off her, and walked away.

They had abandoned me, left me there to die.

Harry had appeared beside me, lying there dead. I needed someone to help me, to hold me, to tell me it was okay and that I was safe with him. But as much as I shook him and shouted at him, the pool of blood grew larger and he remained silent. He had also deserted me.

I couldn't move on the ground. There was too much pain attacking me at once as the larger bat-eries had their turn. My emotional state had been ripped out from me and thrown around onto a big pile of mess.

Something inside of me changed at that point. Something took away all my self-pity, sorrow, anguish and, well, love, and turned it into pure hate and disgust. And I don't mean normal hatred, like, mega evil hatred. It was like nothing I had ever experienced before, no other feeling could match it. I felt like I was…someone else. I looked down at my box of matches on the floor and quickly bent over to get them. As I tried to light the match, I noticed the strangest thing. My left hand fingers had become long and my fingernails cut sharp. I couldn't feel the warm fiery glow in my chest, but instead it was ice cold. I felt jittery and there were sparks on the ends of my fingers. In my other hand I had a steady glow going, but in my left, I had the power over electricity. And then I remembered. My biggest fear ever and will always be, is becoming just like Zacheri, the awful excuse for a human being he was. I could feel the static running through my hair and I knew there wasn't much time left until the effects of the bat-eries venom faded and this fear would go away. At first I threw the fire to trick him into dodging it. And then I did something that I hope never to do again in my whole life.

The energy that pulsated through my body felt like I was being hit by a tsunami over and over again inside me, it was so strong and so hyper. The electricity was spreading down to my legs and I was starting to get scared that Zach would notice my change of state so I quickly moved into action. I didn't know how to power the electricity; I just thought it was point and shoot. But it was much more than that. You had to make sure you were in the same frame of mind as the buzz. Aim it right where you want it to go; with fire you just shoot it and it kind of... fans out.

I leapt forward with a vicious snarl and aimed my outstretched fingers at Zach. He fell to the ground, with me on top of him, half shivering in surprise and shock. I sucker punched him in the nose again and again, until my own knuckles started to bleed. I got up off of him and threw bolt after bolt. There was no stopping my anger.

As the power faded, my breathing steadied. But my bubbling temper did not subside. There were some many things I needed to know, that only he could tell me. I held him down with my foot on his neck. He gagged and choked but had no strength to throw me off.

"Where is GG?"

"I-"

"Where!?"

"She is far, far away. You will never find her." He managed a sarcastic, evil grin that quickly turned into a tormented and distorted cringe.

"So you do know where she is!"

"Of course, of course. Why do you think I would tell you anything, I-"

Another voice cut him off. "She is over there." Angus's voice was very deep and quiet. I couldn't see him at first, he was huddling in the dark corner. He pointed to a small passage I hadn't noticed before. It was narrow and dark and I didn't know if I could trust the burly man.

"Why are you helping me?"

He didn't say anything for a long time. I opened my mouth to ask again but he got there before me.

"Because…because I was a friend of your father's… a long, long time ago."

"Wha-" Smoke started, I put more pressure on his neck so he couldn't speak.

I had so many questions crowding around my head. So many questions that Angus could possibly answer. Like 'Where are my parents?' and 'How can I find them?' I felt almost giddy, despite the fact that there was an evil maniac lying underneath me and that my only friend in the world was dead.

Blinding light beamed out of Zacheri's fingers. It hit Angus right in the heart, a perfect shot, leaving his body jittering and jumpy for several minutes, even after he was dead. I ran to his side and couldn't do anything. If I touched him, I would get shocked as well.

"Why didn't you just use that on me?" I quivered with frustration.

"Because now you'll have to live with never knowing what happened to your parents," His voice shook, "and I think that will be much more painful than dying."

"Zacheri Smoke... why would you do this?"

"I am Zacheri Smoke and I triumph again. I win."

And he breathed his last breath.

GG FOUND

There was no time to waste. I ran down the narrow cave passageway as fast as I could. It winded, twisted and curved. Everything ranked of sizzling flesh and the stench seemed to follow me through the dark tunnels. It made me want to throw up.

I had just killed someone. In fact more than one someone. And I felt horrible. Although, I had to remember that I was a giant leap frog closer to saving all humanity, so that kind of made me feel better. Maybe I could save the world from all evil, maybe I could free the Ice Empress. And maybe, just maybe, I could bring Harry back. It was a long shot, but maybe it was possible for the Empress to bring him back to life. I ran faster and faster down the corridor and almost rushed past a small circular entrance into another dark corridor. I darted inside. My heart raced and so did my feet, even though I had a killer limp and a swollen leg.

As I came through the entrance I realized I was in a warm red room. My eyes swept around the walls and I almost didn't see the tiny barred animal cage, in which GG lay, curled up in a frail little ball. She appeared to be awake; her eyes were open, although she didn't look at me when I stood in front of her. I felt like crying, although I had done quite enough of that already. She was in shock, her arm was contorted in an unusual way, and all of her visible skin was either scraped, cut, or bruised. GG's face was blank and empty of emotion. She was being strong no matter what. I had a feeling that she wouldn't make it back home.

I swatted that thought out of my head, and worked on breaking open the padlock on the cage door. It was no use trying to break it open with a rock or anything by force (it was one of those master locks), and it would have taken too long to pick it. I dragged my fingers through my now black and burnt hair, when I realized how hot my hands were. They didn't hurt me, of course, but I wondered if they were hot enough to melt the metal. I gingerly grabbed the giant hinges of the door and pulled hard. After five and a half minutes, the bolts started to loosen and I could feel the metal becoming softer in my hands. Eventually, the door swung open and I carefully dragged GG out. She moaned a little so I stopped and she lay on the ground, maneuvering herself back into a ball.

"Come on, GG. Wake up. I need you, wake up!"

She groaned in reply. But after a few minutes she slowly slumped herself up onto the shoulder of her good arm.

"What is it this time, Angus? What torture device has Zacheri given you? I've told you time and time again, you will never find out where the key is. Never." She slurred her way through her speech, but seemed more sure on the last word.

"What key? My key?" Again, a million questions came to mind, but I thought I should probably tell her that it wasn't Angus that time. "It's not Angus, GG, it's me. Alexis, your granddaughter. I've come to set the Ice Empress free. Everything is going to be alright." I smiled reassuringly. Although I didn't feel very reassured myself.

She grimaced as she lifted her neck to look into my eyes. And as we looked at each other, relief drained away my strength. I crouched down and hugged her, forgetting about her injuries. She let out a small yelp and I let go of her. In her eyes, I saw love and relief as well, but there was something else there too. Fear and worry, and pain. Lots of pain.

"Oh, Alexis, my dear," she exclaimed, "I've been so worried. But I am so proud of you, you made it all the way here, I knew you could."

I had to tell her about Harry, but I couldn't bring myself to do it. She was already in so much pain. Although I think she already knew something bad had happened to him, because she didn't ask where he was.

We hobbled and limped slowly back to the opening of the cave where the four dead men lay. As soon as GG saw Harry's body, she collapsed and started crying hysterically. Part of me desperately wanted to join her, but instead I walked to the entrance of the cave and looked out at the now dark sky. The wind blew and made the sand dance far below me, I could see for miles and miles. My once short hair had grown almost below my shoulders and I ran my fingers through the tangled mess. As GG cried over Harry's dead body, I wondered when this would all be over. When would I be home and safe? No more exploding mountains, no more ghosts in boats, just safe and sound at home.

A large sob from behind reminded me that if I wanted to get back home, I had to find the Ice Empress. Turning around, I saw that GG was hugging Harry's body, shaking with misery and covered in his blood. I crept forwards not wanting to alarm her, and tapped her shoulder.

"GG, I have to go," I whispered softly. I opened my mouth to say it again because I thought she didn't hear me, but before anything came out, she answered in a croaky voice.

"You must. You must get the last Ice Arrow and then find the Ice Empress and bring her here. She might be able to save him." She turned to look at me, and I never noticed how blue her eyes were before that moment, such a deep blue, like the sea or coral. They were so lonely.

I couldn't bring myself to say 'goodbye' so instead I said, "see you later." GG said nothing in response.

I found my bag near where Zacheri had been sitting and amazingly the first two arrows were still in it, along with the diary. I grabbed the Arrows and retraced my steps back into the mountain, continuing down the winding corridor and passed the room where I found GG. As I rubbed sweat out of my eyes, I noticed I was crying. I almost laughed when I thought of what Lola would say if she saw me crying. Something like, "Such a wimp, child. You're wasting water. Keep moving or give me 200." Although they weren't the most encouraging quotes, it made me think of home and of all the people there, even though I didn't have many friends. Okay, I had none. But they were all still important to me. The whole world is important to me, because it was put in my hands. I broke into a jog, and then into a run.

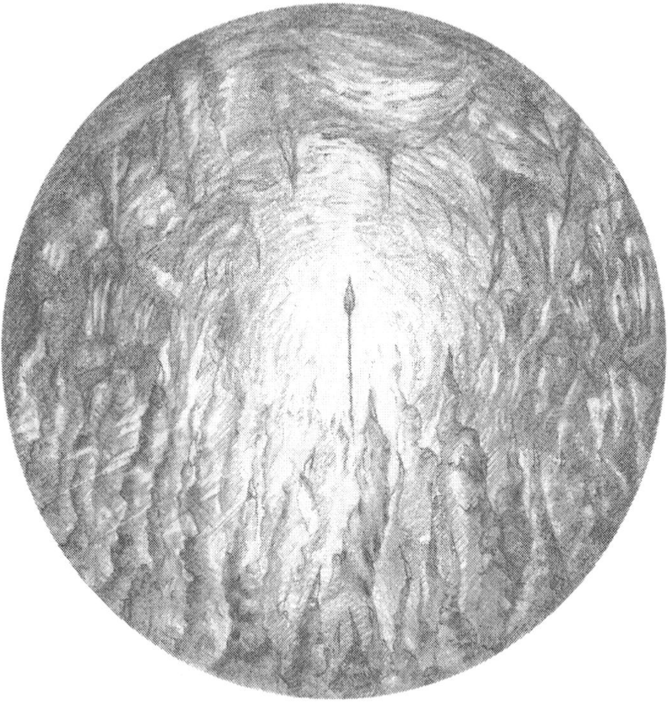

THE CARNIVOROUS CAVE

The room was bright, lit up with torches on all the wall space. The whole ceiling was completely covered in stabbing cones and all over the floor were stinging spikes. I said out loud the words I had memorized from the book; "Right in the middle of the cave is the prize. The golden Arrow." I wanted to run to it but I knew that it wasn't worth the risk of getting attacked by the spiky things. They seemed to spit and hiss as I slowly maneuvered my way through the maze. Not only did I have to watch my footing, I had to be wary of the ceiling. I was beginning to swell up as the spikes got me, falling all over the place, underneath and on top of the evil points. After the sixth time, I swore to myself that I would be more careful. Eventually, I reached the centre. The Arrow seemed to glow in the light of the torches and burned amber and beautiful. Once I reached it, it was surprisingly easy to take it in my hands. I held on to it tightly, along with the other two Arrows, as I crept towards a dark patch without any torches that seemed to be an exit at the end of the pointy maze.

Suddenly out of nowhere a most extraordinary thing happened. One of the stalactites hanging from the ceiling grew larger and larger, absorbing the other stalactites around it to grow. There was no way around it except for a small slip between two of the stalagmites, but going that way I would not be able to avoid being stung. *I could go underneath it,* I thought to myself, but quickly pushed the suggestion aside. But as I stepped towards the narrow escape, the thought crept back into my conscious. *If I slide really fast underneath, it won't get at me,* I decided. I cautiously found a route to build up momentum and began to run. I tripped over a couple of rocks but regained my balance quickly. And too soon for my liking, I slid under the giant spike. Everything seemed to flow in slow motion and I could hear my heart beat loudly in my throat. I almost cheered as my body slowly passed the tip of the spike. And then my rejoicing came to an abrupt halt when my foot hit a rock on the floor and jolted my slide to a stop. The Stabbing Stalactite seemed to take in an audible breath before it pounced its sharp end towards my terrified face.

I AM THE FLAME

I shuddered. I felt the sharp tip dig into my shoulder blade and the burn in my throat from the scream I let out as it pulled out its blade. It poised for a second attack, and I closed my eyes for another round of agony. I felt like it was definitely going to be my last round. And it was.

The lids of my eyes sank down and my breathing gradually slowed. The stalactite aimed for my stomach, but only left a mere scratch, as my body was pulled away from under its wrath by warmth I knew only too well. A warmth that wrapped itself around me and concealed me in its safety. Somewhere in my subconscious, my mind had decided that I couldn't give up yet, that I needed to be rescued. As the pain in my shoulder slowly eased, I smiled up at my best friend, the one that I loved and the one that would always be alive and burning in my heart. Fire.

The room had gone dark, except for one light. Me. The fire had engulfed me, I was a walking, talking flame I felt empowered and alive, nothing could stop me. I walked over to the giant stalactite and sneered. Although the piece of rock couldn't hear me, I teased, "Who's more powerful now? You little piece of rock.

You want a piece of me?" And then I shut up quickly because realized how stupid I sounded. Out of embarrassment, I looked down at the ground and turned out to be standing over a puddle of blood I had left on the floor. My reflection astonished me.

I could see a beautiful flame rising up from the ground, flicking and jumping in all directions. She no longer had the disgusting black tangled hair, but had gorgeous brown bob cut locks, with streaks of orange and bright red. My eyes glowed through the fire like headlights.

Then I saw my shoulder. Although the pain had eased off quite a lot, it came back as soon as I saw it. I could feel once more the deep knife piercing through me and I screamed. I grabbed the Arrows from the floor where I had dropped them and ran. I ran down the next corridor, a breeze swooping through my hair and my agonizing wound. The corridor walls started to get lighter and before I knew it, the walls were white as snow. I was running through a tunnel of ice. As I got further and further down this white tunnel, my shoulder was oozing and I could feel the melting ice dripping onto my head and slowly extinguishing my fire. I raced even faster to escape to the water. I was nearly wading in it by the time I saw the light at the end of the cold hall. All I could think of was going ahead, if the pain in my shoulder had wriggled into my mind I would have crumbled. The light was accelerating towards me, and then suddenly it engulfed my path; it was pure white, so bright that I doubled over and shielded my eyes with my knees. I cowered for what felt like a lifetime, and even when I lifted my head slightly, I had to blink and squint to make out my surroundings. I was in a shimmering palace. There were glimmering chandeliers down the middle of the high, shining ceiling. The walls were covered in beautiful swirling designs, cut out of the ice by hand. And at the end of the room, a door. There is no way to describe that door; it was just mesmerizing. And huge. Directly in the middle of the door was a simple lock. So simple and ugly, it was almost as if it didn't belong.

I took in the whole room, breathing heavily. I still had immense pain in my shoulder, so getting up was a challenge in itself. I didn't even want to think about my task ahead.

I slowly turned around and what I saw almost pushed me over again.

SHOOTING

A tremendous throne strewn with icy flowers: roses, lilies and irises, stood tall at the other end of the room. Above the throne was the target. I picked up the bow sitting by the throne and limped over to the marked spot on the floor. I took my position. I hadn't examined the silver Arrow very much before and it was beautiful. I brought my bow and Arrow up to the right stance and cringed. It was almost physically impossible to get in the right position without pulling my shoulder. I screamed. I would have to use my left arm to pull back the string. I had never shot an Arrow like this before and had never planned on being ambidextrous.

The first shot barely went further than a couple of metres. Again, I picked up the Arrow and positioned myself. It hurt so much the tears started to roll down my face. It was too hard. The Arrow slashed through the air making a piercing noise. I closed my eyes and hoped. A satisfying thud eased my anxiety. First I opened my right eye slightly and gave out a gasp of relief. I had hit it right in the middle, a perfect shot. I felt like jumping up down, but I was too surprised (and it would have hurt too much). It wasn't possible. Maybe just the presence of the Arrows had somehow woken up a part of the Empress and she had assisted the Arrow to its target. I hurried to pick up the second Arrow, the bronze, not paying much attention to my shoulder any more. The adrenaline had eased the pain. I pulled the bowstring back and the Arrow sprung forward. A loud clang signified the entrance of the bronze Arrow into the target, right beside the silver. My confidence grew and grew, I could do it, I could save the world! Finally, I reached for the gold Arrow. As soon as my fingers touched it, a thundering crack came from above. A drop of ice cold water dripped on my nose and I slowly raised my head. The white chandelier was quickly melting away; it must have been my uncontrollable body heat. It was right above where I had to shoot from. There was no choice but to move quickly, I snatched the Arrow and raced into position, nearly slipping. I was shaking like a tree in a thunder storm. Another crack made me jump and drop the Arrow. I was wasting valuable time.

I pulled the bow back but before I could shoot the Arrow, there was a third and final crash, I watched as the colossal chandelier came plummeting down over my head. I let go of the Arrow and was pushed aside, hitting my head against the cold hard floor, oblivious of the result of my last chance effort to save the world.

I had woken up but it felt like I was still in a faraway dream. The walls seemed to shake and the air around me was hazy and smoky. The ground was dry and there was no sign of the chandelier. The throne still stood tall and the target, oh the target... stuck deep into the centre of the target were the three ice

Arrows. The silver, the bronze, and the gold. I broke out into large sobs. I had done it. But where was the Ice Empress, the one who I had come here to bring back to life? As soon as the question came to mind, a soft voice quietly whispered, "Alexis Blake, stand up." I slowly got up and turned to face her. She was a picture of exquisite beauty, flowing hair with a slightly blue tinge that became her long white gown that had a train that stretched two metres behind her. Her eyes were deep, yet icy blue like topaz gems. Her face was perfectly angular and she had lips the colour of ripe strawberries.

"Are you... are you the Ice Empress?" I stammered out the stupidest question on earth, who else would she be?

"Yes," She coolly replied, "thank you for returning me to this world."

"Um...no problem..."

I felt like I was in the presence of royalty. I gave her a really awkward curtsy that looked more like I was bending over to touch my toes. She smiled and returned a grand curtsy that made ripples go down through her dress. As she bowed her head, I noticed her beautiful crown of crystal placed delicately on her glossy hair.

The room seemed to sparkle even more now that she stood in the middle of it. She slowly glided around it, caressing the walls and the beautiful throne. "This place has been my home for thousands of years, though I haven't been able to walk around and touch it. It really is beautiful isn't it?" I mumbled out a quiet agreement. It really was spectacular. She closed her eyes and turned her face away from me. After a few moments of silence she turned to me. She looked as if she were crying.

"We must return to your home at once, so that your bravery does not go unrewarded."

I continued to cry, I was so happy. Finally I could go home and not have to go through another day of fighting off the bad guys or trekking through deserts.

"But first," my heart sank dreading her saying there was another task to undertake, "we must go get your friend."

HOME

I knelt beside Harry and the waterworks started yet again. I reckoned it was a good idea to take him back and bury him at home. I mean, I couldn't just leave him in that cave to rot. Although how were we going to carry him all the way back? GG came and sat beside me. She had already cried herself dry. As if she read my mind (I felt a slight twinge of de ja vu), she whispered quietly, "The Empress said that she can transport us back home. We won't have to carry him."

I nodded and looked down at the ground, "Okay."

"My name is Jesili. You don't have to always refer to me as the Empress," She said softly behind us, "and we wouldn't have to carry him home anyway."

"I...I don't understand." GG's face curled up into a ball of confusion.

Jesili didn't say anything else; she walked around Harry and knelt beside him. At first it looked like she was going to kiss him, but she didn't. She ran a long finger around the rim of his face and stood up.

After a long pause I saw Harry's eyes flutter slightly. I couldn't help but sob even louder. Then he let out a loud scream of pain, he grasped his wound and rolled around on the floor in pain. If I hadn't been witnessing a resurrection, I might have laughed at it. Both GG and the Empress were trying to calm him down with 'shushes' and 'it's alrights'. I just stood back. I couldn't believe my eyes.

I stared at the Ice Empress in fear, if she could bring a person back to life, think of the power she had to do anything she wanted.

But then the walls disappeared and I was embraced by a spinning world of nothing.

I could see Harry in this space-like dimension looking as surprised as I was. My limbs were paralyzed and I couldn't even speak. So this was what teleporting was like? I started to feel a little sick and dizzy, but when I fell backwards, I fell onto my bed at home. In my own room. In my own town.

Apparently I slept for a whole week. On about the third day, people started to get worried. I guess the news of the return of the Ice Empress and the story of our journey got around town pretty fast. Whilst I was oblivious to everything around me thank you gifts and notes arrived by the sack full. Some had been left by my bed, so when I eventually woke I reached for them and browsed. One of them read:

Dear Alexis Blake,

Thank you for saving the world. I'm your number one fan. I think it was really cool how you saved the Empress and I was wondering if someday you could teach me some of your cool tricks, like taking out all those bad guys and shooting arrows and playing with fire. When I grow up, I wanna be just like you. You are my hero.

Lots of love from your bestest friend ever,

Talicia, Age 6 and a half.

Wow. I had never been someone's hero before. It was quite exciting. Then it hit me. I was back home, I was alive and so was Harry. I had killed people and had saved the world. Wow.

I got dressed slowly, like it was just a normal day, and casually trotted down the steps to the kitchen where GG and Harry were drinking tea.

"Good morning," I said as I walked right passed them and opened the fridge door. I grabbed a drink and leant against the counter. We were quiet.

Then out of nowhere, they both got up simultaneously and squeezed me to death. It was nice. I was happy to be back. And so were they. They filled me in on everything that had happened while I was asleep. The Empress had taken our town under her wing and the community was working on building her a home. Zoal built a bridge over the valley so that our two towns could unite together. It turned out many people in Zoal were longing to get rid of the evil Zacheri Smoke. And that was that. Fairly simple. At that point in the story, Lola burst through the doors and ran at me. At first I thought she was going to hit me, because that would be a reasonable explanation for the charging, but instead she snatched me up into the biggest hug I have ever had. It felt good.

The town was alive with colour and sound. The people were happy, singing and dancing. It was like a flipping musical. There were banners out, a big banquet table in the middle of the town centre, and music blasting from every single shop. At the other side of the table there was a massive throne, much like the one in the ice room. She sat there happy and content, watching the people prepare for our arrival at the celebration. Harry stood next to me, nervous and twitching. He looked different in a suit, more grown up. His hair was green today. I think throughout our journey together I hardly ever noticed his rainbow hair. He looked like a super spy that was hung head first in a vat of green goo. His face was the same colour. "Dude, what's your problem? It's no big deal," I teased.

"Are you kidding me, that is a friggin' HUGE deal!"

"You can't be serious, you are scared of this? After everything we've been through, you are scared of a party? Man, get some balls." We both chuckled. "Plus, I should be the one that's scared, I hate wearing stupid dresses." GG had picked it out for me; it was a lilac dress which was way too short for my liking, and far too many frilly bits. I pulled at it, trying to make it go past my knees but it just sprang back up.

"Hey, stop it, you look really nice." He smiled. Well that was a bit awkward.

We all sat around the huge table which was overloaded with mountains of food. Harry was stuffing his face with pork and pasta and fruit. I guess even after a week he was still hungry. I don't know how many times I told the people what happened. I think it got shorter and shorter every time I explained it. GG was having a ball, chatting away. The Ice

Empress was cool and collected, wearing a beautiful light blue gown that looked like a river flowing around the throne. Everyone was so happy. And I was too. But there was still something inside of me that wasn't completely content. There were still questions to be answered. The key around my neck felt heavier and I looked down to inspect it. It was clean and glowing. I think Harry noticed my puzzlement and touched my hand. He moved his head to motion away from the party. We silently crept away from the chaos.

Harry and I walked along the edge of the field and talked. It had been a while since we had just talked. In fact, I don't think we had ever had a proper conversation. The subject wasn't exactly lighthearted. He talked about what his experience of death was like. Dark and full of nothingness as if it wasn't yet time to pass on. Then we talked about what we were going to do now that we were back. We had no idea.

"There is one other thing that we didn't mention to you. Something that happened while you were asleep." Harry said.

"Well go on then, tell me."

"I, um, lost my powers. I guess when death came a-knocking, he took them away." He looked like he was about to cry. I didn't really know how to comfort him, so I just awkwardly patted him on the back. Harry without his shape-shifting powers? It would take some getting used to.

Harry looked down at me. We stopped and he just stared at me for a while. I thought he was going to kiss me for a second. But then he turned around and looked at the sunset. It was a beautiful crimson and pink sky, with orange clouds stitched into it like a beautiful quilt.

"It's amazing isn't it?" I sighed. Yes, it really was.

Printed in Great Britain
by Amazon.co.uk, Ltd.,
Marston Gate.